W9-DEW-837

Advance Praise for The Rampant

"*The Rampant* is one of the most original Apocalypse tales I've read in ages. Julie C. Day avoids cliché and gives the reader the end-times by way of Sumerian myth—except this particular end-of-the-world stalls when one of its principal players decides not to show up. What unfolds is a journey into the underworld filled with joy and horror, hope and loss. It's a wise and lovely story—exactly what I've come to expect from Day."

> —Nathan Ballingrud, winner of the Shirley Jackson Award; shortlisted for the World Fantasy, British Fantasy, and Bram Stoker Awards.

"I loved the epic journey of our two teenaged lesbian heroes, Gillian and Emelia, through the sprawling horrors of the Sumerian afterworld. The clash of their modern feminist sensibilities with the cruel and rigid theocracy of the very oldest gods out-weirds much of the New Weird. In *The Rampant*, Julie Day calls us to visit a fantastical landscape in a voice that is hers alone."

> —James Patrick Kelly, winner of the Hugo, Nebula, and Locus awards

"*The Rampant* was so much fun to read! Is that the right way to blurb a horror novel? I don't know, but it's the truth. Julie Day's novel is smart, playful, sly and, yes, horrifying too. A short gem of a book."

> —Victor LaValle, author of *The Changeling*; winner of the World Fantasy, Shirley Jackson, and British Fantasy awards.

"The girl-powered post-apocalyptic Sumerian underworld quest I didn't know I needed."

> —Sarah Pinsker, winner of the Nebula and the Theodore Sturgeon Memorial Award

Conversation Pieces

A Small Paperback Series from Aqueduct Press

Subscriptions available: www.aqueductpress.com

About the Aqueduct Press
Conversation Pieces Series

The feminist engaged with sf is passionately interested in challenging the way things are, passionately determined to understand how everything works. It is my constant sense of our feminist-sf present as a grand conversation that enables me to trace its existence into the past and from there see its trajectory extending into our future. A genealogy for feminist sf would not constitute a chart depicting direct lineages but would offer us an ever-shifting, fluid mosaic, the individual tiles of which we will probably only ever partially access. What could be more in the spirit of feminist sf than to conceptualize a genealogy that explicitly manifests our own communities across not only space but also time?

Aqueduct's small paperback series, Conversation Pieces, aims to both document and facilitate the "grand conversation." The Conversation Pieces series presents a wide variety of texts, including short fiction (which may not always be sf and may not necessarily even be feminist), essays, speeches, manifestoes, poetry, interviews, correspondence, and group discussions. Many of the texts are reprinted material, but some are new. The grand conversation reaches at least as far back as Mary Shelley and extends, in our speculations and visions, into the continually created future. In Jonathan Goldberg's words, "To look forward to the history that will be, one must look at and retell the history that has been told." And that is what Conversation Pieces is all about.

L. Timmel Duchamp

Jonathan Goldberg, "The History That Will Be" in Louise Fradenburg and Carla Freccero, eds., *Premodern Sexualities* (New York and London: Routledge, 1996)

Conversation Pieces
Volume 69

The Rampant

by
Julie C. Day

Published by Aqueduct Press
PO Box 95787
Seattle, WA 98145-2787
www.aqueductpress.com

ISBN: 978-1-61976-169-8

Cover illustration: iStock.com/Marcel Strelow

Original Block Print of Mary Shelley by Justin Kempton:
www.writersmugs.com

Printed in the USA by Applied Digital Imaging

Acknowledgments

This story started its journey while I was a student in the Stonecoast MFA program, though it took more than a little while to find its end. I'd like to thank Liz Hand and Jim Kelly who read that first, incomplete draft. They gave me both the confidence to continue and the understanding that I needed to set it aside until I was ready.

To Patrick Cahn and Jesse Fulkerson-Cahn, my haven. I always feel welcome in both your home and your hearts. To Tom, Fina, and Holden who believe in my work even when I'm less than sure. To my parents, Claire & Eric Day, my brother, Andy Day, and my oldest friend, Pam Long, who lived some of this with me. To the Post-Apocalyptic Writers' Society (PAWS), for both feedback and friendship. To Joe McDermott without whom this book would never have found its true end. His unflagging friendship kept me pushing forward. To Paul Jessup, Georgina Bruce, and Matt Kressel, who sanity-checked the final draft. My equilibrium thanks you.

And to Timmi Duchamp and Kath Wilham for finding something of worth in this story.

My life is full of the wondrous. When I fail to take note, that is all on me. If I've forgotten to mention your name, you deserve all my thanks whether it's written down or not.

To my father, Eric Day. You taught me the both the power of bold thinking and of calm in the face of sea-tipping disaster. You also conveyed something even more fundamental: we are all travelers in our own life-until-death adventure. I love you dearly.

Chapter 1

The seven evil gods, death-dealing and fearless are they,
The seven evil gods, like a flood, fall upon the land,
Like a storm, they rise, do they,
Before the gleaming Sin, they set themselves angrily;

  —from the sixteenth table of the
  "Evil Demon Series"

[*The Devil and Evil Spirits of Babylonia*, London 1903]

July, Aboveground

Screaming is pretty standard at my house, and tonight is no exception. As I tell Mel way too often, "Another night another nightmare. Baby, bring on the end of the world." At this point, I'm lucky all she gives me in return is an eye roll. Even friendship has its limits.

I take a breath, smell the candle wax of my bedroom shrine. Definitely awake. The summer's hot, humid air is like a familiar blanket pressed against my nose and mouth. The weighted darkness of my bed's canopy is just as suffocating. And then there are the tears. I've been sleep-crying again. At least there are no more screams, though my room isn't entirely silent. There's a banging sound, and a voice.

"Gillian, will you open the fucking window?" Mel. It feels like she's been repeating the same words for a while now. Mel's bedroom is only twenty feet from mine. Pabst cans, leftovers from her father's old stash, are scattered all over the side yard between our houses. Once again, she's outside at night looking way too much like a willing sacrifice and some monster's late-night supper.

Mel is the sister I never had and the best-of-all-possible friends. Mel with her long, dark hair and that half-ironic smile. Whether it's here in Decatur, Indiana, or down in the Netherworld, I know she'll always have my back. Forget the moon; it's way too close. I love that girl all the way to Nibiru and back again. Not that any of us are exactly sure of Nibiru's location.

It's ten years since the hordes of old-world gods, the Anunna and Anunnaki, and all their various demi-gods arrived to kick off the Rapture. The chosen, we're told, will ascend to Nibiru, the home of the King of Heaven and Earth, and join the pantheon of gods as His anointed human servants. As it turns out, life's best of possible outcomes is cleaning up after some sharp-beaked god with a craving for live offerings. And even that promise is a dud.

The Rapture is like a birthday party your parents never get around to throwing. Ten years in and I still get up, brush my teeth, and wonder if today is going to be the day. Then each night I say my prayers before my bedroom shrine, ignore that poster above my bed—a supposed cross-section of the earth: crust, mantle, and all the rest—then fall asleep, and dream. Some nights I travel beneath the earth to the Plains and a purgatory of broken and dead bodies, other nights I drift along the Hubur River on a bone and sinew boat, and then there are the nights I reach the Netherworld itself—the land of the perfectly preserved dead. Incomplete human corpses and godly types might be denied entry, but some nights a living person can dream themselves to the Netherworld, especially if they have one particular god's invitation.

Like tonight.

Tonight was Netherworld Central. The odors were classic: there was something sickly-sweet and rancid, like rotting fat, and something else close to the biting stench of burning hair. But the visions were worse. Tonight I stood in the Rampant's very own mud-brick house. Through an open window, I could see a woman trapped on the other side of the compound's circular moat, a river of red liquid dripping from her arms. A dead woman, obviously. This is the Netherworld, after all. Even in my sleep, it was easy to imagine the jagged gashes that went along with all that blood.

"My baby," the woman moaned. "Alistair, Mommy's here!"

Some things I wish I didn't know. Despite her perfect corpse, despite the fact that she'd actually pulled it off and reached the Netherworld, that woman's mission was doomed before she even arrived.

Pastor Edwins never mentions it, but I've seen the truth. Human babies arrive in the Netherworld as young magpie hatchlings with black-and-yellow beaks—no arms or mouths. Give them enough time and they eventually learn to fly, but that's it. In the afterlife, babies are birds forever more. Amen. That woman wasn't getting her Alistair back, no matter what elegant death rite she employed to travel down.

I force back that dark and familiar sense of shame. Unlike the woman and her lost baby, all I have to do is open my eyes and I'm back in my own bed.

"Gillian, come on." Mel sounds impatient. "Open the window. It's dark out here, and you know I smell delicious."

I untangle my legs from the cotton sheets and force myself to sit up. "Delicious my ass. You better have brought some fucking beer." I reach for my bedside candle, then realize my mistake.

Indiana is gods-damn hot. Like every other summer night, tonight—after anointing the screen with oil—I'd left the window open.

In most ways I'm a good little Sumerian Revivalist. I generally trust in my prayers and the blessed screen to keep the monsters at bay. But I haven't lasted ten years without learning a few things; demi-gods are unearthly mimics. Just because the voice sounds like Mel doesn't mean the creature standing outside my window isn't some squiggled-out monster looking for a midnight snack. It doesn't even mean Mel is still alive, another thought I ruthlessly slap away. PTSD used to be a crippling illness. Now trauma is the norm, and raging anxiety is one of our world's almost-sins. As our Sunday School teachers are always telling us, big feelings get in the way of the important stuff, like trying to stay alive.

I reach down next to my bed, searching for my pastor-blessed knife and supplication mat. Basic Salvation training. Knife first, always, no matter how much worry you're forcing down. Death by minor deity is just a plain bad way to go. Still, despite the ritual's life-saving practicalities, all that freely offered blood and begging have always struck me as incredibly pathetic. If I were a god, I'd eat the loud ones straight off, if only to stop their wailing.

Mat and knife ready, I finally light my bedside candle. The flame's glow shows me everything I need to know.

The window's mesh screen separates Mel's face into tiny metal squares. Some squares show sections of eye, others show the wisps of long, black hair that clings to her cheeks. Each of those stacked, metal-boxed Mels looks poised to hurl themselves out into the darkness and shatter into a multitude of pieces. Anything to avoid the pain.

"You look like a tiny bomb-face about to explode," I say as I swing my legs onto the wooden floor. The kind of thought I only share with Mel.

"Tiny bomb-face," she snorts. "Maybe you really did drink all the empties out here." Mel pushes up against the screen's metal frame. "I mean it, Gillian. Give me a hand."

"'K." The screen shudders in protest as I unclasp the spring-loaded latch and push.

"You need to oil this screen with WD-40, not that church shit," Mel says, not for the first time, as she hands me her backpack, which is thankfully full of clinking cans.

"You need to stop wandering the neighborhood at night," I say, meaning it. A dead and dismembered Mel seems more likely all the time.

In addition to our secret group project, Mel is on her own mission, one she refuses to discuss. It's obvious all the same. Two years in, Mel is still trying to find bits of her dad, any bits, in the hope of adding them to his grave.

Another truth I could do without: only whole, perfect bodies make it beyond the purgatory of the underworld's Plains and on to the actual Netherworld. Despite all the bullshit his children pull up top, the King of Heaven and Earth doesn't like his corpses full-on damaged. The hypocrite. With digestion and all the rest, even if Mel came across the gods who ate Mr. Bareilles, it's a hopeless cause. In the gods' eyes, Mr. Bareilles will always be imperfect.

While Mel closes the screen, I set the candle next to my bedside shrine and slip on my old, royal blue Colts hat. I used to think it would bring me luck. At sixteen I know better, but it still feels good to pretend. To be honest, it feels better than good. "Here's to the end of the world and no more bad dreams," I say.

Mel knows the drill. She doesn't mention the lingering tears on my face. Instead, she claps her hands together and smiles. "Amen. Ready to kick off the Rapture?"

"Let's do it." Tears wiped, I pull our planning notebook out from underneath my mattress and adjust the angle of my hat. "Rapture planning engaged." Our parents would freak if they knew what we were up to. Heads down and stoic is what it's all about these days, if you want to survive anyway. Doesn't matter the gods' big Rapture party is stalled. Those assholes take exception to the idea that they need a human's help with anything. And the Rapture is their most holy of messed-up holies. Yet another reason Mel and I need a solid plan; a pissed-off god, really a pissed-off anyone with power, equals nothing but bad news.

"How about we just skip the prayer book?" Mel has settled on my bed, back against the wall. She's doing that one-eyebrow-raised thing that is all Mel. The room is dim enough that it hides my sudden blush. Probably. Mel's always been tall and skinny like her dad, but these days willowy describes her even better. Sometime in the last couple of years the girl found her curves. Lately, I've had to add these non-friend feelings to the list of things best sealed away. Some nights, like tonight, I'm more like a sieve.

Mr. Bareilles was kind of hot, at least that's what Aunt Cecilia used to say. And Mel is, too, in a girl sort of way. As well as her height, Mel has that Bareilles hair that kinks when it gets long and the light brown skin that tans dark in summer. Me, I'm more of the short, pale, Colts-hat-wearing wallflower type—with delusions of world-ending grandeur. Not that it matters: romantic love isn't part of the god-ordained, post-Ascension lifestyle.

"Earth to Gillian? What do you think? Leave the prayer book?" Mel pulls a beer from her backpack. "We only have so much room in our packs, and that book is huge." As she talks, she restlessly flicks the can's tabbed-top with her thumb and forefinger.

"Okay. Yeah. It's out." Even with the extra thin Bible-paper, the Sumerian Revivalist prayer book is a heavy lift, twelve inches tall and at least six inches deep. Plus, its contents are as irritating as fuck. Gods are, predictably, huge egotists. Each one requires a special series of prayers and invocations, some of which can take hours to perform. And it's not like all that work is a guaranteed save. Those prayers aren't worth shit if a god happens to be bored or hungry, which these days is most of the time.

Forget the four horsemen of Biblical fame. It turns out the MCs at the end of the world are the seven Evil Messengers aka the Rampant and his six siblings. The Rampant's brothers, six of those seven Messengers, arrived ten years ago, ready to wave the Rapture starting flag, just as the King of Heaven and Earth had scripted. The Rampant, however, had other plans. Ten years later that guy's still a no show. But being godly means the Rampant still makes his presence known.

Nightmare messages. What else would you expect from an Evil Messenger. And for whatever reason, he just won't shut up. The Rampant tells me missing his cue was a huge mistake. The Rampant tells me he's stuck. Once I fall asleep the Rampant pulls my dream-self down below. Bedtime has become a night pass to the land of the dead.

Silver-lining time: despite the horrors, my travels have given me hope.

Forget the waiting, or praying, or trying to get those godly invocations right. Mel and I have an actual work-able plan to fix things. The two of us are going to escort the Rampant above ground and kickoff the Rapture. Wholesale perfect deaths for everyone along with a home in either Niburi or the Netherworld, that's the pitch. For some reason, the Rampant keeps adding the Netherworld to our list of Rapturous, post-Earth options, which none of the texts or pastors mention, but whatever. Compared to our current lives, either of those resting places sounds like heaven.

Pain and years-long terror has given me some fucked-up wisdom: gods are way too comfortable with those lies of omission. And the Rampant hasn't exactly bothered to share his entire plan with me, despite all the dreams. That's okay. Once we're down in the Netherworld, there'll be plenty of time for questions: like why he blew off his scheduled ascension and why he needs my specific help. I know who I am. I'm Gillian Halkey, just another living sixteen-year-old girl who's fucking pissed off with our god-created universe.

One thing I'm sure of: gods shouldn't get to call all the shots. What with Mel and all her crazy nighttime wandering, I've made one crucial change to the plan. Forget waiting for the Rampant to finish laying out all his precious details one nightmare at a time. Mel and I are heading down now. The two of us have survived here for ten years, surrounded by the King of Heaven and Earth's Sumerian horde. We can manage whatever Rampant details are left undone. Ruthless demons,

At least I hope so. Truth is, the only thing that's going to stop Mel's night-wandering is this mission, so off we go. Saving what's left of humanity isn't worth shit if Mel isn't a part of the crowd.

The Small Catechism
[of the Sumerian Revivalist Church]

To all faithful and upright pastors and preachers.
Grace, mercy, and peace in our God,
the King of Heaven and Earth,
and in all his godly and demi-godly children.

The Realms of the Dead

Introduction

If you are going to go down to the Plains, let me advise you! It is one of many kingdoms in my realm.

Question: Does God, the King of Heaven and Earth, rule over more than one realm?

Answer: Yes, the King of Heaven and Earth rules over all four realms.

The Four Realms

1. Nibiru, the home of the King of Heaven and Earth.

2. Living Earth.

3. The Plains of the imperfect dead.

4. The Netherworld

Question: Will the sun or the stars ever appear over the Plains of the imperfect dead?

Answer: No. The King of Heaven and Earth resides in Nibiru in his many-roomed home. He is surrounded by the gods he cherishes most. On that final day, He will bless those human servants who are pure of heart and allow them entry to his heavenly realm. The Plains contain only those who have failed him.

Question: Can the imperfect dead cross from the Plains into the Netherworld?

Answer: No, the waters of the Hubur prevent all residents (gods, demi-gods, and the imperfect dead) from leaving the Plains and entering the Netherworld.

Chapter 2

The river of the nether world produces no water,
no water is drunk from it. The fields of the nether
world produce no grain, no flour is eaten from it....
Great holy one, [Ereshkigal], praising you is sweet.

—from "Ninjiczida's journey to the nether world"

[The Electronic Text Corpus of Sumerian Literature,
Oxford University]

July, Aboveground

Mel doesn't just look like her dad. She has his same sense
of humor.

When he was alive Mr. Bareilles kept a little statue of
Catrina, the female Day of the Dead skeleton, next to
their family altar. Not exactly regulation Sumerian Revivalist, but close enough. The statue wore a gown with
a plunging neckline, the breast bones thrust out just as
though they were still covered by two rounded breasts.
It was one of the first things Mel's mom got rid of once
Mr. Bareilles disappeared. Mel said her mom didn't want
to think about who Mr. Bareilles might be meeting in his
new, very physical afterlife. It was a joke—mostly. Even
before the failed Rapture, Mrs. Bareilles was the kind of
person who thought pretty women were bitches and du-
tiful daughters should attempt the background fade. In
this god-fearing world, female insecurity is just one of

the many ritual sacrifices women and girls are expected to perform.

Mel gave up on fixing things with her mom long ago, and now that her dad is gone, all Mel thinks about is Mr. Bareille's imperfect afterlife and the moments before his death. "We made it home from school just fine. We still do," she tells me yet again, like somehow it's our fault Mr. Bareilles didn't want us to attempt the half-mile trip alone. Love is one fucked-up drug, I think but don't actually say. Mr. Bareilles, well, the guy overflowed with it.

I remember that twisted-gut feeling as Mel and I stared through the reinforced glass of the school's office window. I remember the way I avoided mentioning that Mr. Bareilles had never been late before. And the shame-filled sour taste in my mouth: I was glad Mel and I were safe inside.

The rest of the school had already sprinted or skulked their way along the edges of the street, most of them without a parent in tow. Mr. Bareilles was one of the few child-escorting exceptions. Eight years of waiting for the Rapture, surrounded by a bunch of angry gods and demi-gods, wears on a person, especially a parent-type person.

Neither Mel nor I said anything as we watched the fliers circling just past the school's overgrown playing fields. Neither of us mentioned how the demi-gods kept wheeling higher and higher, as though their business with that particular patch of earth was done. Another unpleasant fact left unsaid: our own street was in the same direction, just a little farther on.

The silence could only keep us safe for so long. When the school's two secretaries finally left for the day, locking up the school, Mel and I had no choice, we had to walk home.

It took us over an hour to pick up all those de-fleshed bones. There were tears, sure, and retching, but Mel didn't go for help and neither did I. Leaving meant losing more of Mr. Bareilles's remains. In this pre-Rapture world, scavenger gods are totally a thing.

"Love made Bareilles reckless." That's what my dad said later that night. "It's not like he could have done much to protect you two." Dad sat on his plaid recliner, both his legs propped up on the cushion, his left one and the right one with the mangled foot. Mom sat next to me on the worn brown couch. Of course, she squeezed my hand, a seeming comfort, but she also didn't disagree.

Reality check, this Rapture kickoff plan isn't just for me and Mel. We all need this hell-on-earth to end. Our neighbors, our parents, those secretaries at school: everyone is a tiny bomb-face, a fragmenting person ready to explode. Whole-corpse death is less certain every day, which means more of our dead, no matter how loved, land in the Plains. Among the Rapture's many self-evident advantages: after the living world ends, there'll be no more de-fleshed bones. In fact, there'll be no fresh corpses of any kind. Maybe Mom will even be happier in the afterlife. Maybe everyone will.

I know god-directed dreams are no way to plan an Ascension, but our other options are even more shady, second-and-third-hand bullshit. Besides my Rampant dreams, our main source of underworld information is the twelfth tablet of the *Epic of Gilgamesh* and a fragment of Sumerian poetry entitled "In those days, in those far-off days," translated, of course, by Sumerian and Akkadian language experts who've never actually spoken a word. Unbelievable. Ten years after the great religious pivot, somehow the historians and priests think they have this whole Sumerian Revival thing figured out.

The Netherworld, the so-called experts tell us, can only be reached in two ways: (1) if a living person finds one of those gods-guarded doorways described in scripture and then walks on down, or (2) if a living person dies and people bury their entire rotting remains, preferably underneath their family home. Yeah—nasty.

Mel and I are counting on another option we've christened Option 1a: busting our way through some very carefully mapped-out cracks that the Rampant has tracked down. If the Rampant is wrong, if I've miscalculated or misunderstood, we could be stuck in the Plains forever. In other words, we could die. Our late-night planning sessions feel more than worth the loss of sleep.

"Socks?" Mel prods as I look over our packing list. Rule #5 is all about footwear.

"Socks," I agree. "Though I really think we need to consider each of the rules in order—" I pause as I catch a rustling of branches in the pines that separate our two yards. Dethroned Jesus and the holy gods. With Mel having crossed the window's barrier, my anointed screen is no longer entirely god-proof. I drop the notebook and dive for the window as Mel cracks open a beer and tosses it my way. In a one-two motion, I open the screen and hurl that can toward the pines, the window's protesting metal frame be damned. There's a snap of tree limbs as the monster-of-the-week bends to retrieve its prize. My two favorite godly vices: laziness and greed.

"Let's finish this plan, yah?" Mel says after the creature's shambling footsteps finally disappear. She grins at me. "Time to drag the Rampant up to Indiana and ascend the fuck out of here." Mel is so damn badass. That smile of hers, it gets me every time.

"Sure." I lick flecks of beer foam from my hand and smile back. "Still don't get the appeal of the Blue Ribbon beer. It tastes like watered-down piss."

"What immortal wouldn't want seriously skunked Pabst?" Mel snickers, and suddenly I feel as though the world isn't an entirely lost cause. That's one of my favorite thing about Emilia Bareilles, her stupid keep-going heart.

"The first rule?" I prompt. It's time to get our Rapture review on.

According to *Gilgamesh*, there are six rules living travelers must follow when visiting the Netherworld. Six rules may not seem like much, but parsing each one, no matter how potentially lifesaving, is also a huge pain in the ass.

"Do not carry weapons?" Mel asks.

"Yeah, the extra stupid one." The same thing I say every time. As far as I'm concerned, that first law of the Netherworld is totally idiotic. The human body is one giant arsenal. Perhaps the gods expect us to hobble toothless and fingerless into the afterlife. More likely they don't expect anyone to even attempt the journey. The silence demanded by rule number two supposedly makes the entire trip a non-starter.

Stupid, stupid gods. Living people always test the rules, at least until death sneaks up on us and we're trapped— just as the King of Heaven and Earth intended.

The Small Catechism
[of the Sumerian Revivalist Church]

To all faithful and upright pastors and preachers.
Grace, mercy, and peace in our God, the King of
Heaven and Earth,
and in all his godly and demi-godly children.

The Six Rules for the Living

Introduction

If you are going to go down to the Netherworld, let me advise you! My instructions should be followed. Let me talk to you! My words should be followed!

Question: Where do these rules apply?

Answer: In all the realms of the underworld.

The Six Rules

1. He must not carry any weapons.

2. He must not make any noise.

3. He must not wear clean clothes.

4. He must not behave in a normal manner toward his family.

5. He must not wear sandals.

6. He must not douse himself with "good" oil

Question: What are the consequences if these rules are not adhered to?

Answer: Loss of the self, the final death.

Chapter 3

Raging storms, evil gods are they
Ruthless demons,
who in heaven's vault were created, are they,
Workers of evil are they,
They lift up the head to evil, every day to evil
Destruction to work.
Of these seven the first is the South Wind

   —from the sixteenth table of the
   "Evil Demon Series"

[*The Devil and Evil Spirits of Babylonia*,
London 1903]

August, Aboveground

The history of the Sumer Empire is drowning in firsts. It was the first of the Mesopotamian empires. The first culture to write down its stories and myths. The first culture to build a city. Set along the Persian Gulf, Eridu had canals and a temple and boundary stones. It overflowed with clay tablets that recorded the history of its gods. Later came the Babylonians and Assyrians with their re-woven stories, but the source of everything is Sumer and the fragments they left behind, ugly, body-part-and-pain-central stuff. Our modern world, for all its flaws, used to be so much better than all of that.

The Rampant has made me a promise. If Mel and I get things sorted, this old-school, earthly existence will end. Sometimes life—or human existence—just sucks. At least with the Rapture there'll be no more culling of living humans and no more bored gods playing pickup games of mid-day terror. Like all godly gifts, even this sliver of relief has its price. In the end, we still have to play by their rules.

To kick off the end of days, Mel and I have to physically travel to the Netherworld and collect the Rampant, the King of Heaven and Earth's final Evil Messenger.

Tonight is the night. Ready or not, Rampant, here we come.

It's dusk. Low-hanging clouds obscure the sky. I'm hunkered inside the shrubs at the back of my yard, sweltering in my chosen underworld uniform—jeans and a hoodie—while I cradle the glass jar full of corn borer moths. The moths bang against their glass cage in a frenzy of fluttering wings, as though desperate to find their way underground. Crazy as it seems, I'm counting on that being the literal truth. If it all goes to shit, the moths will help guide us back to the surface. They're part of my homegrown GPS and also a totally stellar backup plan despite Mel's complaints of "overly complicated" and "not entirely thought through."

From inside my house, I can hear Reverend D'Ambrosio, the superstar televangelist of the Rapture Age, on our TV. "The Rampant, the last of the King of Heaven and Earth's Seven Messengers is almost here," the Reverend bellows. "Woe unto those who have not yet found salvation." It's been almost two weeks since the last power outage, and like every other electricity-night, Dad is trying to find redemption from the depths of his Lay-Z-Boy. Of course he is. With that half-eaten foot, the Rapture is Dad's only chance of a decent afterlife. We all know the Netherworld is never going to take him. The King of Heaven and Earth has his standards.

Meanwhile out here in the real world, there's a leathery smack of air against desiccated flesh.

"Offspring," the godly creature shrieks or, perhaps, "offering." Beaks, even of the consecrated variety, just aren't made for human speech.

Our backdoor slams open. "Gillian Halkey, you get inside here right now." It's Mom. She looks all sorts of wrong with those stringy arms and her over-sized t-shirt. Mom used to be all rounded thighs and soft, soft arms. Yet another thing eminent salvation has managed to fuck up. All pleasures, food and otherwise, are now off limits.

"Blessed are the pure of heart," Mom tells me way too often. "For they shall see God the King." Running it through the mom translator is not a heavy lift. She means no sex, no boyfriends—or girlfriends, I guess. No un-sanctified desires of any kind. That's the deal if I want to float up with the rest of the chosen and clean up the King of Heaven and Earth's beaky messes. The sad truth is I actually agree with her. Our best bet is a Rapturous ascension and chores without end. Amen.

Mom flicks on the porch light as somewhere overhead a beak-throttled voice cries out, "Gilliannnn."

"Honor your mother and father, Emilia." Mrs. Bareilles yells, from their neighboring house. There are more words, too low to make out, and then the sound of shattering glass.

"Emiliaaaa," the flier cries. A scrabbling sound follows as a shadow lands across our roofline.

Mom flinches and turns toward the open backdoor. "Bob, we've got a visitor. Gillian—"

"Hon, just shut the door," Dad says. "Gillian's probably over at Mel's."

"I really don't think so."

"Then Vernie's perhaps." Another Dad fail. Vernie and I haven't hung out in years.

"Damn it, Gillian." For a long moment, Mom stares out into the night, and then she's gone, hidden once more behind our oil-sanctified backdoor.

Sometimes life is the worst. I wish I could follow her, wrap my hands around her too thin arms and tell her I love her just the way she is. Pull out of one those card games she still likes to play. Instead, tonight Mel and I are staging our very own underworld intervention. Corpses and tunnels for the win.

From my spot in the bushes I watch a beam of light cross Mel's yard just before Mel emerges from the pines.

"Gillian?" A fresh bruise runs along her right cheek, obvious even in her flashlight's uncertain glow.

"Over here. Move fast." Careful, careful, careful: those Camp Hallelujah lessons are a worn track that won't shut up. Doesn't make them any less true.

As Mel steps closer, I notice the pick and length of rope hanging from the outside loops of her backpack, just like we planned and listed in the notebook. What we most definitely didn't plan is the container of bacon that she's currently holding. Mel must have pulled it from some special corner of her kitchen.

"Bacon? Really?" I say, trying for funny.

"It never hurts to be prepared." Mel's expression is definitely not amused.

"Okay. You're right. Prepared is good." I try not to think about what else she may have hidden inside her backpack besides this saltiest of security blankets. Though really, bacon couldn't make things any worse. If Mel hasn't figured out that a few servings of bacon aren't going to placate all the creatures of the Plains, I'm not going to be the one to tell her. Instead, I hand Mel the moth jar, slip on my own backpack, ignore the snake of fear closing up my throat, followed by the rush of self-doubt. "This is it, my friend. Time to head on down."

It's then that I hear a thud, followed by the sound of leather against air. With two tasty humans out in the open, the flier has finally committed; it's dinner time.

Mel and I, though, we're children of the Rapture—ten years in. We know exactly what to do.

As we run, the beam from Mel's flashlight bobs across the patchy ground, toward the lilac bush in the far corner of the yard and the entrance to our homemade tunnel. Despite my own backpack and heavy boots, I'm pushing hard, forcing myself not to pause or look back.

"Faster," Mel snaps. Her legs are keeping pace with mine, though I know she could easily outrun me. That's my Mel, loyal to the end, gods-damn her.

"Faster," a laughing voice echoes from behind me—way too close.

I push forward: one step, two steps. And then something slams into my right side, hard, knocking me to the ground. Careful, careful, careful. Hold in that scream. I can taste dust and scraps of dried grass. My backpack seems to be dragging me behind it as the flier pulls me across the yard. And still I don't make a sound.

The Rampant wouldn't let me die before I'd gotten beyond my own backyard. That's what I tell myself, trying to ignore a less comforting fact: the Rampant doesn't know that we're actually heading down tonight. That particular communication failure is all on me.

"Offering!" Mel shrieks. "Offering."

It feels like the whole neighborhood must have heard her, though not a single adult comes running. Mom would charge right out that backdoor if she heard my voice, but that's not going to happen. A dead mother is definitely not on my wish list. There are already too many familiar people waiting for us in the lands of the dead.

I try to roll onto my back, try to pull away, and for some reason the flier actually lets go. I can see the dark shadow of my house against the starless sky. I can feel the cool glass of the moth jar in my hands. I can even feel my chest moving. Okay, so definitely, astonishingly not dead.

"I cannot fucking believe this." It must be the shock. The words are out of my mouth before I have a chance to think them through.

Mel is crouched off to my right, slowly backing in my direction. The flier stands a few feet beyond Mel. His legs may end in talons, but his arms are muscular and totally human. His face, in the thin beam of Mel's flashlight, is nothing but sharp beak. Pretty standard for the demi-god set. The real surprise is Mel's slab of bacon. The stupid bacon, all shiny with fat, but no more than a half a pound tops, hangs from one side of his demi-god beak.

The King of Heaven and Earth may have sanctified his godly and demi-godly children, but he didn't give them an equal measure of brains. I outweigh that salted meat by more than one hundred to one.

"You okay?" Mel says, turning the flashlight in my direction. She has that thin-lipped expression that means she's terrified but not about to cop to it.

"No way is a slab of bacon as much of a meal as me."

"Christ, Gillian. *That's* the take-home message?"

I lean one hand against the dry earth and lever myself up. My back and legs, even my ass, hurt. There are going to be bruises. But I'm alive. "Let's just go, okay?"

"Okay."

Why does she always have to be so fucking reasonable?

With the flier busy, we head to the back corner of the yard and slip behind the lilac bush. My last view is of the flier's chest and throat thrusting forward as he gulps down his prize.

On the other side of the bush sits the homemade cover to our tunnel, the center of our daytime encampment for the last six months, our very own Camp Callus. Mel sets the flashlight on the ground, and the two of us swing the cover open. Inside rests the familiar aluminum ladder. A rope runs down from a hook we screwed into the center board, our own jury-rigged mechanism for reclosing the trapdoor while we work. Hungry gods and demi-gods are one of the few constants in this non-Rapturous world.

"Ready?"

"Yeah."

"Do you want me to go first—" I start.

"Nah." Mel grabs the flashlight, and just like that, she's climbing down, leaving me with one backpack and one glass jar.

"Mel, Gods-damn it. What about the moths?"

"Your makes-no-sense GPS?"

"Half GPS," I reply. "The other half involves the caterpillars."

"Exactly."

"Mel, we need a fucking backup plan, and this is the best I could come up with." I set the moths down next to me and toss my backpack into the hole. There's an *oof* and then a dull thud as the bag hits the dirt floor. Shit.

"Gillian, was that on purpose?"

"No, you idiot. Of course not." I take my first step down, grasping the jar in my left hand while I cling to the ladder with my right. Why did I choose glass? Plastic may be modern and sinful and all, but at least it's practical.

The jar could so easily slip and smash, losing the moth-half of my special jury-rigged guidance system.

"Gillian?"

"Coming." I step down, releasing my left elbow and reaching with my right hand to grab the next rung.

"I've got it," I crow just before the jar slips from my fingers, and then there's the sound of shattering glass. A beam of light flares up from below.

"Broken," Mel says.

"No." I don't like the edge of panic in my voice. I'm definitely not supposed to be this scared.

"Look, it's okay. We just need to keep going. Follow the plan." Mel sounds so calm and steady. She sounds like the girl I've known all my life, the one who sticks it out no matter what.

What else can I do in the face of her bullshit and bravery; I lower myself down, counting the rungs as I go. Seven. Six. Five. Four—

"I've got you," Mel says as her hands slide around my waist. And then she's lifting me and setting me on ground.

"Tall is good," I say as way of a thank you. I can feel my face flushing, which thank gods I'm pretty sure she can't see. Being touched by Mel didn't used to make me feel this way. "Mel, did the moths—"

"All fly ahead? Yeah."

I try to ignore the length of Mel's body next to mine and focus on our surroundings.

Mel's flashlight illuminates the tunnel we've dug in the hole's southern wall and the holy army of corn borer caterpillars that wriggles up from the depths. Those caterpillars are the Rampant's living breadcrumbs and the second half of my oh-so-complicated, organic GPS. Having godly powers has its perks. The Rampant has cursed those newborn insects with an obsession. The caterpillars are determined to find their way to the surface and our Indiana corn fields. Lucky for us, their quest creates a living, wriggling trail. Mel and I can follow that mass of caterpillars all the way to their underworld hatching grounds.

Even without the glass jar, the caterpillar half of our GPS plan is still intact. Once we collect the Rampant and return to their hatching grounds, that path of caterpillars will lead us home. My glass jar covers our return journey before that point. The Rampant's corn borer moths are compelled to find their underworld hatching grounds and lay their eggs. With my jar, all Mel and I had to do was watch which way our trapped moths tried to fly and head in that direction: Netherworld moths to Plains hatching ground, Plains hatching ground and caterpillars to the surface. Not exactly a foolproof plan, but still.

Without the moths, tracking our way back to that underworld field and all its caterpillar breadcrumbs—finding our way home—is going to rely entirely on the Rampant and one ugly little word: faith. No backups. No backing out. Nothing but barreling all the way down.

"Let's do this," Mel says, then grabs the rope and pulls the cover shut.

"Me first." Before she can argue, I slip on my pack, try to kick the worst of the glass out of my way, and start crawling. The swinging beam of Mel's flashlight follows me, highlighting the jagged clots of earth that form the tunnel walls and the sea of brown-and-red caterpillar heads. I can't help it. With every movement forward, I crush more baby caterpillars, destroying their dreams of aboveground cornfields and sun-blessed leaves.

Crawling isn't so hard. That's what I tell myself. I try not to think about things like elevated carbon dioxide levels, try not to notice the dank and earthy air. For a while there's only the sliding of our blue-jeaned knees against the packed earth, the sprays of dirt that tumble against my neck and head. The uneven ground that grinds into my knees.

"Stage one complete." Through the flashlight-powered shadows, I see our first goal, the cleared-off section of the concrete drainage pipe, a few feet ahead. The pipe marks the end of our homemade tunnel and the real starting point of our journey. Despite our weeks of work, the opening we chiseled into the pipe's concrete side looks so damn small.

"Gillian, you said the caterpillars stop once we leave the pipe and reach the hatching grounds?"

"They hatch in the field near the pipe and head to the surface." I agree.

"Once we cross the Hubur River and all that how exactly *are* we going to find our way back? With the moths gone, a bit of a backup plan would be nice."

"Ha, so I was right? Overly complicated, my ass." I always thought my moth plan was more than a bit of a stretch. Except that the jar is broken and the moths are gone, and total faith in anything godly seems somewhere between suicidal and insane.

"So? How is it going to work?"

"We'll stick with Plan A: the Rampant and his godly power will guide us home." My voice is all indignant. Maybe if I push back hard enough, Mel won't notice just how worried I really am. Truth is, I'm not convinced the Rampant really cares where we end up. I don't even know if I'm the only person trying to travel down. Nightmares are a disjointed mode of communication and a really convenient excuse for letting some details fall through the cracks.

Heat lightning is common here in the Midwest. Summers when they weren't watching TV, Mom and Dad used to sit out at night with a beer in hand, watching the clouds spark one against the other. But around my sixth birthday, chaos descended. Funnel clouds formed over the Midwest. Tornadoes razed huge sections of Kansas and Missouri along with bits of Illinois and my own state of Indiana. It was tornado season times one thousand. The waters of Lake Monroe were sucked up and dropped sixty miles north in Indianapolis, the closest our state's got to Sodom and Gomorrah. The debris field was large enough to drive people into their Midwestern, concrete-pour basements. On my birthday, instead of shaking off the summer heat with a swim down at Farrigan Beach, Mel and I huddled inside the wooden cupboard at the far end of my family's cellar.

"Doesn't scare me," Mel said every time another roll of thunder shuddered across the sky, chased by an ugly crack of lightning. It was dark inside the cupboard. I could feel the hairs on my arms standing on end. I could smell the acrid stench of ozone along with the familiar cedar chips and mothballs. Mel squeezed my hand. "I'll stay with you, though. Until you're ready to go back upstairs."

"I'm fine," I said. "I like dark places." Which wasn't entirely untrue

Though we didn't know it then, the weather was supposed to be the Rapture's heraldic call. Along with the tornadoes, the gods, demi-gods, and most of the Seven Evil Messengers were in transit. The Rampant, though, kept his distance. Rapture Interruptus.

Of course the Apocalyptic weather didn't last long. Once all those immortal types realized they were stuck here, the holy storms settled right back down. Turns out, a godly rager isn't much fun when you have to actually live with the consequences.

"I'm so brave," I say now, trying not to think about all of the dead waiting for us at the other end of the tunnel. Little Rebecca Chavis's entire life was spent with no memories of the time before. Our almost-Rapture world was her entire life, and then just like that, it was over. Mel and I are still alive. We still have a chance at something better. It suddenly feels like such an ugly accomplishment.

I slip off my pack and slide it ahead of me, through the hole we've chiseled and into the drainage pipe. There's a strange echoing thud as the bag hits the concrete floor. Darkness and a musty scent of decaying leaves seep out of the opening. I adjust my lucky Colts hat—feel that dopamine surge of safe, safe, safe spreading through my brain—and turn to Mel. In the flashlight's beam, two corn borer caterpillars crawl along the back of my hand, their black heads and brown bodies speckled with honey-colored flecks. "Breadcrumbs. Pretty, pretty breadcrumbs." I announce in my best third-rate magician voice. I even manage a cheesy grin

"You're totally the bravest of the brave." Mel says, smiling at me. It's not just those willing sacrifices some gods go on about: the pureness of the offering and all that. There's power in old knit hats and carefully placed bravado.

A lot has changed since I turned six, and it's not just the almost-Rapture. I was the first one to try out our lawnmower Go-Kart. The first one to climb the apricot tree in my front yard and swing up onto the roof. It seems like since that first day, hiding in the dark with Mel, I'm always pretending to be the brave one. With the Rapture almost upon us, fear, my fear, seems beside the point. Forget spiritual rebirth and salvation. These days all that matters about our lives is the quality of our deaths. No wonder we all work so hard to avoid it.

"I'm bringing the caterpillars with us," I say. "At least some of them should get to see why they're doing all this."

"They're not on the list."

"Neither was that damn bacon and whatever else you've added to your pack." No way did Mel stop at illicit meat products.

"Fine. Whatever. We need to move, okay?"

"The voice of reason," I intone, drop the corn borers into a small container. Then it's hands on our crudely chiseled entrance and a dive through the opening into the drainage pipe itself. "Gods-damn it. This hole is really small." I twist and twist again, scraping up my forearms as I shove my right shoulder forward and then finally tumble through to the other side. I land on a bed of yet more insectile foot soldiers that ooze against my skin. "Gods!"

"Gillian?"

"All good." Shafts of light filter down from the pipe's storm drains, but it's not nearly enough. It's gods-damn dark. Fretting is for the weak, I tell myself as I stand. But I'm so full of crap. We're headed to the underworld. We're outside the sanctified entrances to our homes. Anything could happen to us down here. My backpack landed just a few feet away. I unzip it and quickly pull out a can of Pabst. As Pastor Edwins repeats each and every Sunday, the gift of fermented sugars is just as acceptable as blood.

And beer cans are so much easier to open than veins.

"Gillian—"

There's a *snick* as I push down on the can's metal tab and turn. "Don't you come another step—Oh." Gillian Idiot Halkey. While I've been fretting about monsters,

Mel's managed to silently shimmy those skinny hips of hers right on through the concrete opening.

"You look like the underground nightly special." Mel politely refrains from outright laughter as she shines her flashlight on the can of Pabst and the beer dripping down my arm.

I shrug. She's not wrong, but this new cheery version of Mel is all sorts of unsettling. Never mind my own mess, she's dripping with hope.

Mel's flashlight beam moves away from me and out along the length of the passage. The floor of the pipe is covered in the expected carpet of undulating insects. But for some reason a forest's worth of leaves dot the ceiling and walls. "What the—" I reach toward a cluster hanging near my head.

"Don't," Mel says.

Too late. I hear the faint crunch of fragmenting cellulose, and then something thick and gummy splatters across my hand and face: cocoon fragments and metamorphosing caterpillar. "Oh, man. This is so fucking nasty."

Mel snickers. And why not. Beer, bloody scrapes, and now this: I'm a demi-god's wet dream.

"Don't fool yourself, Emilia Bareilles. You're looking almost as tasty. They don't get much living flesh down here."

"True enough." Still cheery. Still not mentioning the reason: her gods-damn dad. "Now why don't you pull something useful from that pack of yours? Like your own flashlight, for example? I don't want mine to run out of juice before we get down there. I'll switch to a candle for a while." She's smiling stupidly, excited even.

Damn. Mel hasn't mentioned her dad, not once. But we both know Mr. Bareilles is somewhere down below. Really and truly the problem is the world, not Mel. In this fucked-up life, hope is like one of these underworld caterpillars, almost certain to get crushed.

Mel tosses me a pair of cotton knee socks from her pack as she digs out a candle for herself. "You should probably clean up."

We chose the socks because of rule number five, but—added bonus—they also make a decent washcloth.

Of God's six rules the Fifth Law is one of the easiest— and most obscure. The living should never wear sandals when visiting the dead. With so much that could go wrong, to me socks seemed the easiest way to make sure we're not misunderstood. Socks are a shoes-only accessory.

Not all parents are broken love-and-joy hoarders. Some of them actively care. If Mel's dad knew what we're up to, he'd be totally furious. Mr. Bareilles used to carry a sharpened umbrella when he walked us home from school, as though the pointy end would actually drive away all the fliers. If the power was out on a Friday, he always begged and borrowed enough gas to run the generator for a couple of hours. Skipping our weekly movie night, he said, was not an option. How else were we going to learn the important stuff? But without Mr. Bareilles, it's hard not to let those lessons fade. Somehow everything feels harder.

Following Mel's directions, I'm carrying my own flashlight while Mel walks ahead of me, holding her own lit candle. We're trying to conserve batteries, but the wavering light cast by the candle is like a stumbling-drunk scout leading us forward. It feels like it's going to disappear at any moment.

Overlaying the fetid air of the concrete pipe, I can smell the bitter scent of crushed insects. "The Rampant is going to be pissed," I say, stepping through a particularly dense pile. "He went to a lot of trouble to hatch these guys and mojo them into their topside obsession."

"They're just trail markers to the Plains. I'm sure he doesn't really care."

"Yeah. Maybe..." All living things are somehow sacred. That's about the only belief that feels authentically my own. But it's not worth arguing about, not while we're belly deep in this end-of-the-world mission, my anxiety bare inches from leaking out. All the effort the Rampant took to raise these baby caterpillars. And now after months of nurturing, the caterpillars are nothing but insect jelly, a death smear wherever Mel and I step. That fleshy bastard god had damn well better care.

In less time than I expected, there are no more storm grates and no more rays of sunlight falling through their bars. And still the caterpillars continue to flow upward, our reverse guides through the labyrinth. Above ground our plan seemed so clearly superior. Never mind finding the actual secret doorways down to the Netherworld created by the King of Heaven and Earth and then dealing with whatever guardians drew the short straw. Never mind dying complete-and-whole like the woman in my dream. All Mel and I have to do is follow the caterpillar stream until we find that crack through to the underworld. But now that it's more than a pencil-and-paper game, our plan doesn't sound simple, it sounds stupidly vague, with a Gillian-the-asshole side of "leaving early."

Scrape. Tap-tap.

"Mel?"

Candle in hand, Mel turns my direction. "The echoes probably make it seem—"

Scrape. Tap-tap. Chitter.

Jesus and the false prophets. Before I manage to even gasp, I'm dangling feet above the ground. A thick slow-moving goop drips down my cheek and into the creases of my neck. My backpack, the backpack still attached to my back, is being held by something above my own head, something that clings to the ceiling. Forgot our Camp Hallelujah training. Calm can go fuck itself. Living or dead, ceiling clinging is definitely not a human trait. Meanwhile Mel, upside-down-walking-on-the-once-floor-now-ceiling Mel, is no longer smiling, no longer careful either. She's dropped her candle and is running toward me while my flashlight spins on the floor like some demented disco ball.

"Mel, don't—"

Creak goes the canvas of my backpack. *Snip, snip,* chitters whatever is overhead.

And I'm not screaming. Focusing all my energy on not screaming. What kind of creature lives in a manmade tunnel, even a manmade tunnel that leads to a crack between the worlds?

Ignoring all sense, Mel leaps, and I howl as her body slams into mine. I'm trapped. My arms are tangled in the pack's straps, straining to hold our combined weight. It feels like they're about to be torn from their sockets.

"Sorry. Sorry. Sorry." Mel's pumping her legs, as she clings to my waist. It's like she's preparing for a dive into the Farrigan River from our old rope swing.

The thing on the ceiling clicks and screeches as it fights to pull me up. Meanwhile, the tug-of-war is messing with our pendulum motion. We're spinning in circles, banging against the tunnel's cement walls. I can't stop the sounds, though my groans and whimpers don't change a thing. The pain is an un-tuned symphony, an assault. Thank gods for cheap manufacturing. My arms slip out as the pack's stitching finally gives way.

It's Mel who falls first, my body landing on top of hers. Both of us sprawl among the caterpillars. My legs, my arms, my lips, every part of me seems to be trembling. In the beam of the slowly spinning flashlight, I watch my pack rise upward: my half of our supplies. All of the liquids, including the beer and water, gone.

I roll off of Mel. She's crying, making short little hiccupping sounds as she sits up and slings her own pack off of her shoulders. A moment later her flashlight shines up toward the ceiling.

"Mel, it's going to be all—Shit."

"Damn," Mel breathes.

The woman hanging from the ceiling is like none of the godly we've come across in our corner of Indiana. Instead of eyebrows, she has black ridges that rise up to her hairline. Her mouth is nothing more than a lipless, half-open hole. She has a crazy amount of arms, though. Some of her arms end in hands while others lead to hardened pincers. I watch as one of those claws tears my pack open and a second one reaches in.

Pastor Edwins has trained me well. I know exactly who this woman is. She's a child of Ninhursag, the goddess of childbirth. She's also a goddess with what has to be one fucked-up backstory. Goddesses aren't supposed to scuttle along a manmade drainage pipe with neither the dead nor the living for company.

I hear the snicking sound of something sharp piercing something metal, then the goddess raises the can to her mouth hole. Ninhursag's daughter is finally knocking-back her hard won beer. "Think she likes flesh with her brew?" I say. At this point, it's bravado or terrorized screams.

"Try to stay quiet." Mel's leaning over my sprawling form. At least she isn't crying anymore, though her voice sounds like some strange mixture of shaken and grim.

"What—" Before I can finish, Mel grabs my upper arms and yanks me to my feet.

It feels like a set of twin lightning bursts has struck my shoulders. I let out a grunt, force the waiting scream back down. Breathe. In. Out. You got this.

"There's four more cans to go," I murmur into the collar of Mel's shirt as she holds me upright, my body wrapped in her embrace. We have four cans worth of potential leeway before Ninhursag's daughter decides on her next move. I can feel Mel's heart thumping, her wet cheek pressing against my hair. She smells of sweat and moist earth and a dusty Mel scent I can't quite define. I don't ever want her to ever let go.

"Your arms—" she finally says. "Sure you're up to this?"

"I fell on top of *you*." I inhale one last time, then take a step back, clench my jaw against the whining pain. "Want me to take a turn with the pack?"

"Nope."

I don't argue. Instead, I turn and start to jog along the pipe, grabbing my still spinning flashlight from the ground and ignoring the sudden wave of nausea that follows. I glance back. Ninhursag's daughter is watching us, beer can in hand, not trying to chase or follow us, not even baring her goddess teeth. Perhaps killing is not her thing. Perhaps that was her problem all along.

After a moment I hear Mel's footfalls trailing my own. The corn borer caterpillars swarm across the floor and the curving walls of the pipe. It's no longer musty. A scent, both sharp and repellently sweet, pervades the air. We're close to the tunnel's end and all those dead people I don't want to meet, like Mr. Bareilles and little Rebecca Chavis.

Rebecca was our responsibility, mine and Mel's. When she disappeared, that dried scalp fragment with her orange hairclip was all they found. And now Rebecca, along with all the other imperfect dead, is trapped in the weird neither-here-nor-there land known as the Plains.

I should never have let go of Becca's hand.

The Small Catechism
[of the Sumerian Revivalist Church]

To all faithful and upright pastors and preachers.
Grace, mercy, and peace in our God,
the King of Heaven and Earth,
and in all his godly and demi-godly children.

The Imperfect Dead

Introduction

"Did you see the spirit of him who has no funerary offerings? How does he fare?"
"He eats the scraps and the crumbs, or he eats not at all!"

Question: Which of the dead are considered imperfect?

Answer: Those who die and are not buried complete and whole are considered imperfect and shall not enter the Netherworld. They shall be cast aside on the Plains.

Imperfect Death

1. He who is not buried.

2. He whose remains are scattered.

3. He who is not mourned.

Question: Do the living have a duty to the dead?

Answer: Yes. God, the King of Heaven and Earth, instructs us to bury our loved ones and to mourn their loss. In return He shall grant them entry to the Netherworld.

Chapter 4

Her voice reached Heaven, her voice reached Earth,
her resounding cry covered the horizon like a
garment, was spread over it like a cloth, she hurled
fierce winds at the head of the cumunda grass
(saying): "Cumunda grass, your name......
You shall be a plant...... You shall be a hateful
plant...... Your name......"

—from "the šumunda grass"

[*The Electronic Text Corpus of Sumerian Literature*,
Oxford University]

Underground

He must not make any noise, the second rule states. What
with breathing and footsteps, it's yet another impossible
requirement. Mel and I tossed it almost immediately. But
it's one thing to call bullshit from a shrine-protected bedroom in southern Indiana. It's another to break a supposed godly law while standing in one of the lands of
the dead.

"Behold the birthplace of our caterpillar guides," I
pause for a beat, waiting to see what if anything shows
up. "Second-rule test complete, I guess." We've finally arrived at the hatching field. Rebecca Chavis, Mr. Bareilles,
and all the rest of the imperfect dead reside beyond the
cave-enclosed field in the actual underworld Plains. After
hundreds and thousands of years of immolation, lost

limbs, and unmourned death, the place has got to be pretty damn full.

"Sure. Test complete," Mel agrees as she uses her flashlight to scan the cave. "Are we really going to turn off the lights?" Her tone doesn't sound relieved. It sounds grim.

"Yeah, we really are. Confirm light source. It's on our list."

"Right."

We're standing at the edge of a shallow, stone basin that ends about a hundred yards away against the cavern's far wall. Both of our flashlights are trained across the open space. The Rampant calls the basin his field of breadcrumbs, and it is. It's full to overflowing with caterpillars.

Behind us rests the drainage pipe and the opening we just crawled through. It took us hours to pick-axe a human-sized hole, expanding the existing crack, though truthfully Mel did most of the work, while I held my flashlight's beam steady and tried to rest my savaged shoulders. Now a torrent of corn borers surges around our legs, heading toward their newly widened exit up to the surface. The caterpillars tumble over each in their frenzy. By morning, tens of thousands of these larvae will feel the sun on their skin for the very first time.

The land of the dead is a total misnomer. In the twin beams of our electric lights, the cave is riotous with life. The ceiling vaults up almost thirty feet, leaving plenty of space for the morphing cloud of magpies and moths that stream back and forth between our edge of the basin and the opposite stone wall. The cloud seems focused on an opening in the far wall that's about eight feet high and just as wide. The living creatures here don't seem to care about our arrival at all. Why would they: we aren't part of their particular Rampant-inspired obsession. In this underground madhouse, moths lay eggs and magpies assist.

"Lights out," Mel whispers.

"Lights out," I repeat, close my eyes, and switch off the flashlight. A total act of faith. I count to ten and re-open my eyes only to find the Rampant really has provided.

Green-glowing bioluminescent mushrooms grow in patches from the cave walls. Their light mixes with a dense constellation of blue dots in the field itself. Life finds a way; this section of the underworld is lit by mushrooms and caterpillar corpses dense with glowing microbes. A bonus science lesson from the Rampant: blue-glowing bacteria like to travel inside parasitic worms. The worms infect our caterpillar guides while the bacteria continue to grow their microscopic families into brightly colored dots of light.

Sights, smells, sounds: the entire cave is filled with the *witter witter witter* of flapping wings and a rustling that rises from the field, similar to the death rattle of dried cornhusks. Those sounds aren't the worst part of this underworld ecosystem. A shadow rain falls down from the swarm of magpie beaks. Even with our flashlight and the bioluminescent glow, it's too dim for me to make out any details, but thanks to the Rampant and his patchy intel, I know exactly what that rain contains. Mel, however, is seeing, smelling, hearing it all for the first time.

"Test complete?" Mel says.

"Yeah, test complete."

Mel switches on her flashlight.

"You know, I really do love you, you idiot," I say, eyeing the nightmare swarm. I can feel myself blushing, but honesty seems like the least I can offer. This isn't a place any living person should visit, dead father or not, and yet here Mel is, standing next to me. Before I even realize what's about to happen, I've pulled my Colts hat off my own head and placed it on Mel's, and then I'm pressing my lips against the corner of her mouth and cheek. A kiss. How did that happen? In the underworld light it's hard to make out Mel's expression. Surprised, maybe. Startled. But definitely not angry. She even reaches out and grabs my hand. We stand like that, on the edge of the unknown. Despite my fear, I trust her.

"Remember that movie?" Mel asks, letting go of my hand.

"The Alfred Hitchcock one with all the birds?"

"Naw, the one with all the high school kids and that crazy killer in the clown mask."

"Yeah."

"Clown masks just don't seem that creepy, you know? Compared to other stuff."

I nod my head and start to bend, intent on examining the growth at the edge of the field, then freeze as starbursts of pain pulse out from my shoulders and crawl right up inside my skull.

"Gillian—"

"I'm fine."

"Right. I can totally see that, my hero friend." Mel scans the ceiling. "So what exactly are those magpies up to?"

Following the movement of an individual bird, their flight path becomes obvious. There are two different types of creatures in that cloud: moths and magpies. Both enter the cavern from the opening in the far wall and fly over the field, but only the magpies return to the opening again. One more air-based constant, something that looks like rain, or perhaps snow, falls over the entire caterpillar field. What interests me right now, though, is the cloud of winged creatures. The opening at the far end of the cavern is getting harder to make out through the thickening swarm. "You know, there seems to be a lot more magpies now than during my Rampant dreams. I guess the field is running low on nutrients."

"What do you mean 'nutrients'?"

"Nothing," I say a little too quickly. One of those lies of omission Pastor Edwins is always talking about.

"Bullshit."

Lie lobbed. Lie caught. Mel knows me too well.

I shake my right leg, dislodging a phalanx of caterpillars intent on invading the bottom of my jeans. "I fucking hate caterpillars."

"Stop avoiding the question and just tell me."

Emilia Bareilles. Even in the lands of the dead she is a total badass. "The magpies are carrying remains, okay. For the newly hatched larvae. Not many food options to choose from down here. It's a lifecycle thing," I try to explain.

"Uh." Mel takes a deep breath. "Gillian, we've talked about this how many times? You said the field was done, as in gods-damned-fucking done."

"Well," I pause. "It's never entirely what you'd call done, not with the constant hatching. The caterpillars are hungry, right? They have to feed before they're ready to travel. Look, this whole deal bugs me, too, Mel," I rush on. "The Rampant's plans make a kind of sense, but he's really more of a sing-along kind of guy. You know: oracular and shit. Straightforward isn't really his strength."

"The sing-along guy *bugs* you?" Mel's voice sounds funny, as though she's frantically trying to hold something inside. She's staring at me, all dark brown eyes and eyelashes that seem to be blinking out some sort of frantic Morse code.

And then stupidly, unexpectedly, she's laughing. We both are, busting up in fact.

"When the heck were Evil Messengers ever any good with detailed plans?" Mel snorts. "For the gods' sake, all the Seven had to do was show up, and the Rampant even managed to get that wrong." And just like that Mel is back: the fear, or anger, or whatever heavy thing she was holding managed.

"Okay then." I push away the drumming pain in my shoulders and shine my flashlight out into the weird-ass field. "Thoughts?" I ask as Mel's light joins mine. The field overflows with lumpy plant-like structures. Clusters of corn borer eggs, like tiny pearlescent sea urchins, cling to the leaves, while stringy tufts, black and rust-colored, lay scattered across the plants and bits of exposed ground. The stringy stuff reminds me of discarded corn tassels. I know it's not. There is no Utu and his rising sun in the Plains. Real corn plants, real plants of any kind, just aren't possible. The Rampant's caterpillars have to settle for a different source of nutrition.

Mel is distracted, still figuring out the next steps in our travel plan. "The magpies are using the same entrance to go in and out," Mel says. "Am I getting that right?"

"Yep. Only one entrance to the Plains for everyone, including us." The only way out of the cave and onto the Plains is across a field of remains and through an eight-by-eight opening filled with Rampant-cursed birds. Though I'm not about to repeat those facts out loud. "Time to move." I start to reach for Mel's hand and then chicken out at the last second. What if it seems too soon, too needy? Instead, I start to sing. Mom used to sing with me on those nights when I was too scared to close my eyes. This time I'm trying to convince myself to keep them open.

Alouette, gentille alouette,

Alouette, je te plumerai.

Lark, nice lark,
Lark, I will pluck you.

I will pluck your eyes. I will pluck your eyes.

And your eyes! And your eyes!
And your beak! And your beak!
And your head! And your head!
Lark! Lark!
O-o-o-oh

Alouette, gentille alouette,
Alouette, je te plumerai.

I move slowly, trying and failing to avoid the flurry of wings, but moving all the same. The ground is no longer bare stone. Instead, it yields under my feet in a way that resembles actual soil. The flying swarm gets denser with each step and so does the special magpie-delivered rain. Something falls against my cheek. Something else brushes my lips. The texture: it feels like hair, long dead girl's hair. Rebecca Chavis and her ponytail and hairclips.

Three years out and I'd almost convinced myself I didn't care. Becca was just so annoying, always moaning about having to stay with us when we walked to school. "Gillian. Mel. I'm not a baby," she'd say as she tried to tug her hand free. She was only seven and I was thirteen; I knew better. But that day I let go anyway. I guess I was sick of her complaints.

The hardest memory: Mel and I sprinting ahead, not waiting to see if Becca would, or could, keep up. In a world full of ugly and wrong, I left a seven-year-old to whatever monsters happened by.

Now I'm walking through a cloud of magpies obsessively seeding a field with desiccated remains. It feels like Becca's skin is falling against my lips, like Becca's glossy black hair is stroking the back of my hand.

I flinch, take another abrupt step forward, and then stop. Even with my eyes open, I can barely see the flashlight in my hand, never mind my feet. My hoodie clings to the sweat now trickling down my back and chest. This isn't under-the-covers scary or watching-movies-in-the-basement scary. We're in the middle of a full-on bird-and-moth storm, edging toward the underworld. "Mel?"

"I'm over here," she replies from somewhere off to my left. "We must be over halfway by now," she continues, her voice stone-cold solid.

"Yeah, it's fine," I reply a little too loudly. "Just keep going." *Really, it's fine,* I repeat to myself. So what if we left a little early. The Rampant created this path. He's the one trying to help us end the world. But there are other truths as well; I aim my flashlight at the ground. The plants grow in an unexpected rainbow of colors: gray-green, purple, orangish-brown. Some are even patterned, swirls of color and curving lines. Tattoos, inked who knows how long ago, decorate the skin-leaves of the Rampant's breadcrumb garden.

I swallow hard, taste bile at the back of my throat.

I know this field makes sense. It's practical even. Mel and I need trail markers, the Rampant's moths need somewhere to lay their eggs, and the corn borer larvae need something to eat before they start their journey. The Rampant has done his best. He's repurposed this land's detritus, its equivalent of shiny gum wrappers and torn plastic shopping bags. It's not his fault that some of those shiny gum wrappers are made from seven-year-old girls.

"Gillian, I think we should stay close," Mel calls out. Her voice quavers this time, a barely perceptible break that pushes at my own calm.

"Head toward my voice," I manage as a length of skin falls across my face. What the ever-loving fuck. "Hoodie time." I reach up and grab the hood of my sweatshirt.

"Covered already, turtle girl."

"Oh." Mel's voice is so damn close. While I've been fumbling with my clothing, she's somehow managed to track me down. In the beam of my flashlight, Mel's black hair hangs down from beneath her burgundy hood. I see a smile flit across her face, and then it's gone. She holds out one hand, palm up, and scowls at the bits of rain landing across her still-living flesh. "Jesus, Gillian—*hair*?"

"Among other things," I say, trying to hide my relief. Thank, the gods, she'd gone with angry, instead of scared.

And then Mel and I are shuffling forward, shoulder to shoulder. Wings are all around us, beaks and claws, too. My arms, my shoulders, everything hurts. Bits of flesh catch on my eyelashes and forehead. Imagined or not, I can smell shampoo, Dove soap, detangling conditioner. It's in this moment that the magpies start their dive-bomber routine. Something scratches my cheek, followed immediately by another scrape just above my left eye.

"Hello. Gillian," a voice calls from somewhere up ahead. Meanwhile, the magpies are screaming: *kkkk ka kkkk ka*. It's that Alfred Hitchcock movie from Mr. Bareilles's movie night after all.

"Mel. *Mel!*" The heel of my left boot catches on something round—skull sized—that crunches, and then gives way. Old, old bone. "Keep walking, damn it," I cry out, unsure if the words are for me or for Mel. *Keep walking.* All that planning. All that work. We are not going to fail. We can't.

"Gillian." The unknown voice calls again. A girl's voice. A child's.

And then someone's wrapping their arms around my head and shoulders, pushing the birds away. The arms are soft and warm and intoxicatingly alive. I recognize the feel of her immediately. It's Mel, my Mel, the two of us clinging to each other as the storm rages. Even in the frenzy, I'm Rapture trained, a straight-A-apocalypse student. Somehow I've managed to keep hold of my flashlight.

"Gillian, could you loosen your arms just a little?"

"Okay." What the hell? Is Mel trying to pretend this holding-me thing wasn't totally mutual? Oh gods, what if she's not so rock solid? What if she's changed her mind? I manage to move all of two inches before Mel tightens her grip.

"Just a little," she clarifies. "I want to peek through the gap between our arms without getting slashed."

"Oh—good thinking."

"I know." That girl, she always could do dry.

I can feel my heart beat slowing from terrified down to merely scared as I wait for Mel to finish her survey. Even in the darkness of our arms, I can tell something has changed. A few magpies still batter against our bodies, but the focus of their rage seems to have shifted.

"You know, it looks like those birds are trying to push the moths back through the entrance." Mel reports.

"Why the fuck would they do that? Let me see." Silently, Mel adjusts the position of her head so I can eyeball the cavern. Of course she's right. A mass of magpies about ten feet away are thrashing about at what seems to be the cave's far wall. Instead of flowing in and out of the entrance, the birds are looping down and around, a never-ending waterfall that blocks the entire opening.

It seems the chaos of that first bombardment was just those birdbrains figuring out their target.

"Gillian, Emilia, follow the sound of my voice," the unknown girl calls from the other side of the storm. She speaks slowly, carefully enunciating each of her words. It's like she doesn't believe Mel and I can figure out how to reach an entrance all of ten feet away.

"Who the fuck is that?" Mel whispers.

"I guess we're about to find out. Come on." And then I'm humming "Alouette," matching my shuffling steps to the song's rhythm. And Mel is humming, as well. The two of us are singing our way through the last of the skin-leaves straight to the entrance and that magpie storm, walking blind inside our tangle of arms.

Even sightless, it's completely obvious when we reach the entrance. The magpies go full-on berserker, claws and beaks thrusting against any body part not covered by clothes, pack, or boots.

Definitely time to push through.

"Hurry," the voice cries over the enraged *kkkk ka kkkk ka* bird chorus. Something dry and leather and unambiguously dead reaches through the flaying wings and grasps my right hand. The dead arm tugs, hard, and just like that Mel and I tumble forward across the bird-covered opening and through to the other side.

"Away from sie door," the girl directs, her so-wrong hand still dragging me forward. *Sie?* When rushed it seems our dead savior speaks English with a German accent. Yet another lesson from Mr. Bareilles and his movie-night specials: *Raiders of the Lost Ark*, or perhaps *The Adventures of Baron Munchausen*.

"You need to do exactly what we tell you—" our would-be savior manages before a second girl interrupts.

"Adala, this isn't how the plan's supposed to go. The Rampant told us to wait until they'd come through."

"And he vas wrong."

"But—"

While the two dead girls argue, Mel's grip tightens on our still intertwined arms, her breath so warm against my cheeks. Not looking, that's the most important thing. The Rampant promised me that some of the dead would help us across the Plains. He didn't mention that their presence would also drown me in scorching vats of shame.

"Gillian, please don't be afraid," the second girl won't stop talking. Even worse, her voice sounds so gods-damn concerned. "It's just that things got all mixed up. Why did you have to be so early? The Rampant said we had months to finish—"

"Now you want to follow the rules?" My words sound so much sharper when spoken out loud. "I didn't mean. That's not— Sorry." And still I don't look, don't pull away from the comforting darkness of Mel's arms.

"Becca?" Mel's voice sounds flat, off. She's ignoring my stupidity, ignoring the dead girls' scheduling concerns. Her body is so still. Perhaps she didn't even notice.

"Yes, it's me."

Rebecca Chavis. It's like pulling off a Band-Aid or a thousand too-old Band-Aids. I'm trying hard—but actually hearing her name—tears leak from my closed eyes. I didn't cry at her funeral. None of us kids did. We called it a special tribute. Now it just seems pathetic and sad.

"Gillian Halkey and Emilia Bareilles, what are you? Ostriches? Open your eyes," the other girl, Adala, demands. She's so damn self-possessed. Up to now I haven't hung out with many dead people. Who knows, maybe they're all like this.

"Right." I finally let go of Mel, open my eyes, even pull off my hood. "Rule number three—"

"Is all set," Mel says, completing my thought. "We so have this covered." She glances over at me, even managing a bit of a smile, as though, inside, she isn't all sorts of terrified. Mel has always been a fucking valiant liar. We both know this isn't much of a win.

Rule number three requires us not to wear clean clothes. Even if we hadn't carefully worn our clothes for three days straight before heading down, they're now coated with once-living bits of human. Turns out, in the lands of the dead *Gilgamesh*'s rule number three is pretty much a gimme.

"Hi, Gillian," Becca says into the sudden silence.

"Hi, Becca."

For whatever reason, the four of us have lined up in the center of the cave, Mel and I facing our two underworld greeters. Looking at Becca, it's far too easy to imagine her last few minutes of life. For the most part Becca's body is made of a sort of spirit flesh, a glowing holographic version of little Rebecca Chavis, but there's a jagged piece of skin, one of the few remnants from her living body, hanging from her left arm. The length of exposed jaw below her left cheek is just as troublesome.

The second girl, Adala, is looking Mel and me over just as carefully. Not that I blame her. Living visitors to the lands of the dead are vanishingly rare. Only the desperate sign up for this particular tour.

My dad says people used to think that those ancient religions were plain ignorant, the Egyptians and their Duat; the Norses' Hel; the Greeks with their Asphodel Meadows and river Styx. Standing in front of Becca and her mummified friend, it's clear all those ancient peoples totally nailed it; both life and death are entangled with the physical.

The cave we're currently inhabiting divides the Rampant's flesh-field from the Plains proper and all those discarded souls. The space might be just a few yards long, but in the bioluminescent-fungi-and-dead-Becca glow, I can see that it's filled with life. Blooms of Lion's Mane mushrooms that look like shaggy sections of fake white fur hang from the walls. They're mixed in with coral-like pink-and-white fungi and clusters of yellow-and-gray button mushrooms. A wilderness of shrieks and moans drifts in from beyond the cave, punctuated by stretches of almost silence. I find the noises—difficult. From the tight-lipped look on Mel's face, she's not doing so well herself.

Skraaaa, a bird-god cries, followed by a scuffling sound and voices, close enough to make out their words. "Not me, gods-damn it. No!" The language and choice of swear words peg the screamer as a recent arrival.

"Gillian. How are we ever going to—" It's Mel.

"Shhh. No way am I dying today, Mel Bareilles. Not here."

"What the—" Mel cuts me a look. "This was your idea."

"It's okay." Becca sounds so calm. "They're not all that close."

Which is probably true, but absolutely no real comfort. I'm finding it hells hard to deal with Becca's glowy little-girl body and milky little-girl eyes.

"Anyway, no one dead likes to get too close to the magpies," Becca continues. "Well, I guess, almost no one." She pauses for a beat. I'm not sure if she's proud or just uncertain of our response. "The Rampant put me and Adala in charge of the boat."

"Boat?" I am such an idiot. We have to cross the Hubur River, the gateway to the Netherworld. Of course we need a boat

Even with that dried leathery face, Adala manages to totally give me the stink eye. "We have collected, bartered, even spent time with the boat builders." There's no mistaking her distaste for this last item. "But your early arrival," she continues, "it is a…complication."

"Huh." And now Adala and I are in some sort of staring contest. That dried little body. Those desiccated eyelids. How often does a dead little girl actually need to blink?

I hear the contents of Mel's backpack clank as she sets it on the ground. *Hhu hu hmm.* Mel makes a soft throat-clearing sound.

"Gillian." It's Becca. "Look."

Damn it. I break first and follow the direction of Becca's pointing hand. Match one to Adala, the Queen of Stares.

A rounded structure, about eight feet in diameter and about three feet tall is set near the left cave wall. Through the cave's green-tinged light, it's easy to identify the boat's building materials. The bone frame is only sparsely covered in sewn-together pieces of leather.

A skeletal frame in more than one sense, I think, somehow managing to keep the dumb joke to myself. Definitely *not* the right moment.

"Gillian, you said it was time to head down. Right?"

"It *was* time."

"Really?" Mel pulls back her own skin-and-hair dusted hood and stares at me, as though she can somehow read my mind, or at least my intentions.

Don't ever fall in love with a girl who's known you your entire life. Her expression. It's like she can recite every lie I've ever told, every lie of omission I've carried inside.

"Mel, I had good—"

"—intentions?" Mel interrupts with that patented Emilia Bareilles frown. "You always do."

"Hey. I know you're upset about your dad, but there's no way he'd want you to risk your damn life. He'd be so angry." Is she really judging me after all I've done?

"Gillian, shut it. Okay? Don't you dare."

If this were anywhere else, anywhere normal, one of us would have stalked off by now. But it's not. It's the fucking land of the dead.

"Stop it. Right now." Becca's tone is fierce, her glowing dead-girl lips a thin grim line. "Girls should stick together, especially down here. That's what Adala and I decided, and that's what we're going to do, help you."

The look on Mel's face is so not good, and each of Becca's words just makes it worse.

"The Rampant asks for a couple of volunteers to help us across the Plains, and you guys say 'sure,' we're the ones for the job? Are all dead people this insane?!" Forget all our calm-and-careful Camp Hallelujah training. Mel is a full-on exploding bomb-face. "Gods. We ditched you, Becca. After we promised your mom. And now you want to help—"

"Please, Mel." Becca doesn't sound angry. She sounds sad, which is so much worse. "I don't want you to end up…" Her voice trails off. "I miss my mom."

"Becca, don't you remember what happened the last time the godly took an interest in you? As far as they're concerned, you're just some still-moving snack."

Becca flinches and takes a step closer to her friend.

"What the fuck, Mel?" I blurt out. That look of horror on Mel's face expresses exactly how I feel. We both know she's gone too far.

In the end it's Adala, rather than Becca, who speaks up first.

"I am four hundred and thirty years old, Emilia Bareilles, not some naive little girl."

"Approximately four hundred and thirty years old," Becca clarifies, as though this is a key difference we all need to understand.

"True." Adala reaches out and squeezes Becca's shoulder, giving her the dried-lip dead-girl version of a smile.

Adala's body. Oh, man. She has two mummified arms and a mummified leg. Her second leg is broken mid-thigh spirit flesh making up the rest. But it's her eyes that really get to me: grayish-blue and seemingly very much alive. Okay, as it turns out, those dried eyelids don't blink all that often, but when they do, a fringe of fair lashes brushes down against her rigid cheeks.

"And I'm not a little girl either, Mel Bareilles." Becca turns and holds my gaze with those shining eyes and that discolored length of jawbone, her expression unyielding. "I'm ten years old. Right, Gillian?"

"Yes, Becca, you're definitely ten," I say. At least she no longer sounds sad. Three years. Rebecca Chavis is three-years-dead. I reach for Mel's hand, the grubby warmth of it. And Mel, my Mel, despite her anger, doesn't pull away. I guess in this place the touch of any living flesh is welcome.

"Mel, since when do big kids hold hands?" Becca asks, as though changing the subject will make all this awfulness better.

"Good question." Mel says, letting go of my hand way too easily and stepping toward the cave's underworld entrance. With her back turned, her expression is completely hidden.

Damn it. Is she scared? Worried? Horrified? Or like me, so fucking jammed up inside she can't even tell?

The cave's opening is about the width and height of a set of church front doors. Unlike me, this is Mel's first view of the Plains. My friend stands so upright as she faces her dad's likely resting place, her hair streaming from the bottom of my Colts hat, wavy and dark and perfect. Painful moment or not, the hat looks way better on her than it ever did on me.

"This is by design? An entry point that includes dead people *and* demi-god fliers?"

Okay, not terrified. Incredulous.

"The fliers are everywhere down here." Becca explains. "Or at least I think so…" There's that doubt again, a little kid lost in the world of the damned.

"They are," Adala confirms with all of her four hundred and thirty years of experience.

"What immortal idiot would piss off the King of Heaven and Earth enough to get tossed down into this hellhole—Shit" Mel glances back at the two dead girls her face twisted in an apologetic grimace. Hurting the feelings of the dead is most definitely not on our to-do list.

"Emilia, how much beer did you bring?" Adala asks, ignoring both the slight and the wordless apology— Ignoring me as well, the person standing right in front of her.

What the hell. I'm the one who had to deal with all those Rampant nightmares. But somehow Mel is our expedition's leader?

"I was liquids." I say a bit too quickly, not giving Mel a chance to respond.

"I don't understand." Adala tilts her head questioningly, a facsimile of friendly, but the angle is all wrong. The stretching of neck and shoulder muscles under resistant, leathery skin—living bodies don't move like that.

"My pack had all our liquids: the beer and the water." I look down at my feet, scuff one of my boots against the ground, focus on the feel of my shod foot against solid ground, anything other than Adala.

"Understood."

I can't help myself. I glance up just in time to see Adala straighten her head back to vertical, a spring-like movement that is far too fast and deeply unsettling. "And Ninhursag's daughter got it all," I continue, finally getting to the relevant point.

"Ah." Deciphering Adala's meaning is easy: once again I've royally fucked up.

"Oh, Gillian." Becca's little face looks stricken. "But your boat isn't ready yet. You really can't drink from the river. It's no good."

"We will just have to acquire another boat." Adala turns, wraps Becca in a stiff almost-hug. "I will be back soon." And then without further consultation, she's stepping past Mel, slipping through the cave entrance, and straight out into the King of Heaven and Earth's designated wasteland. Of course, that damned dead girl explained absolutely nothing.

"Wait! Becca, where's she—?"

"If Adala says it's going to be okay, then it's going to be okay." Becca moves next to me, taking Mel's place, and grasps my hand with one of her own. Becca's spirit flesh is cool and slightly damp, but somehow altogether comforting. It's then that that three-years-dead little girl gives my hand a squeeze. "Gillian, you don't have to be afraid. You won't die like me. I promise."

The air feels suddenly trapped in my throat. Breathing, that's just one of the many things Becca can't do anymore. There is no gateway for Becca, no Netherworld or Niburi. For the imperfect dead this is the final stop. Even if Mel and I succeed, Becca and her friend are stuck here forever and ever. Amen.

"Gillian, you know how Pastor Edwins was always preaching to us about our nightly prayers, and the catechism, and all that stuff?" Somehow Becca manages to sigh with those dead-girl, holographic lungs.

"Sure." That little hand gripping mine. Gods, how many girls like Becca exist in this place entirely bereft of family?

"Gillian, you know what Pastor and all those camp counselors never bothered to explain? Not even once?"

"No. What?" I force myself to ask.

"How to survive if we didn't live to the Ascension. Gillian, being dead really, really sucks." Becca pauses, no doubt checking to see if I'm going to call her out. "Sucks" is prime swearing territory for the seven-year-old set, and Becca's mom was always pretty strict.

"Becca, I'm so friggingdy frig sorry," I say, a sad reach for funny, but it's also true. I am. "How about we take a look at this place?" I add, a lame attempt at distraction.

"Okay." And then Becca's tugging me toward the cave entrance, totally letting me off the hook.

And then it's Becca on my right and Mel on my left, the three of us standing at the entrance to the Plains.

"This place is full of fairy lights," Mel murmurs. She glances at me with a bemused expression.

"Yeah," I agree, giving her this moment.

Out past the shore, the Hubur River contains patchy blooms of algae and dinoflagellates that glow from within their watery home. Closer in, on dry land, clusters of light spread across the Plains. Living insects—click beetles, railroad worms, and fireflies—share their light with the underworld, along with the bioluminescent fungi. This world is a rainbow of blues, reds, yellows, and greens. Even the shimmering forms of the untold dead are like living, flickering jewels.

But I've visited this particular rodeo before, even if it was in my sleep. To our right and left, the dead extend out beyond the horizon. Directly ahead, the Hubur

River is maybe three football-fields-worth-of-bodies away. From this distance I can make out the yellow-white swath of shoreline and, farther out, the handful of boats floating on the river's surface. Though they're nothing but smudged outlines, I know what those boats contain: gods and demi-gods trying to get across the river to the Netherworld, gods and demi-gods continuing to fail. The river is the King of Heaven and Earth's barrier for the unworthy. Dead people and godly types who touch it are all sorts of fucked. As non-residents, Mel and I supposedly can ride that river all the way to the Netherworld. Yet another one of those items we unfortunately have to take on faith.

"Gillian," Mel says, and then nothing more.

About twenty yards from the cave, a group of people have formed a rough circle, holding up what looks like a misshapen trampoline.

"Go ahead," a man's voice directs from somewhere in the ring.

The more holographic bodies in the circle, flexible in a way eons-hardened flesh could never be, lean backward, torsos straight, hands still gripping the lumpy leather cloth. There's a creak that seems all leather and sinew, followed by the pops and cracks of separating bone, and then the trampoline starts to stretch outward. The movement is like too-cold taffy being pulled by some eager little kid. Even with all that effort, the extension is so damn slow.

"More," the trampoline-man groans. Unlike his desiccated body, the man's voice is deep and vibrant.

A secret Rampant-truth I've promised myself I'll never reveal to Mel: in this discarded section of the underworld, no one remains their living self forever. While gods and demi-gods don't ever change, human corpses continue to disintegrate after they leave their graves. Decade after decade, the dead maintain their dried flesh and bits of bone, trying to forestall the inevitable. Some people hermit-crab up, catatonic before the process is complete, others slip into the Hubur River and end it all, and then there are the ones, like this man, determined to use all possible tools to forestall his end. Spend enough years down here and ritualistic pain can become yet another experience to keep your mind focused and whole.

"Gillian, I mean, I love you and all, but what the hell. How am I ever going to find my dad?" Mel sounds more numb than pissed.

And suddenly I'm feeling a little sick. The stupid fucker. She loves me. But she's also not going to give up on her dad.

"Holy Nibiru, Mel, your dad's the reason we're early. All your stupid night walks." A low blow. Mel loves her dad. Getting him out of this hellhole, of course she wants that. But after all those years of pre-Rapture, Mel still hasn't figured out the most basic death-fact: in the real world, even death doesn't last forever. Once a soul disappears from the Plains, it's gone.

"Enough." Mel takes a breath and looks over my head, toward Becca. "Sounds like you guys are working on a new plan. What is it? Details, Becca. Please. Surprises are *not* helpful."

"Okay." Becca looks downright uncomfortable.

Something's up, but all I can think about is how Mel's ignoring me, my Mel, as we stand on the precipice of madness. I try to let it go, try harder as I listen to the silence between us and the trampoline-man calling out yet another command. "Pull. Pull harder." Try even as I watch the writhing mass of dead and desiccated humanity spread before us as far as I can see.

"Mel, there's something you should know…" Becca begins.

"Yeah?"

"Noooo," the words slip out before I can catch myself, and then Mel's turning, staring out at the Plains, following my line of sight toward the thing moving swiftly in our direction.

"Gillian. Do you think?" Mel asks, our fight and just about everything else suddenly forgotten.

A gas-blue flame, human-shaped or at least bipedal—two arms and two legs—is heading toward the cave. The fireball weaves around the dead crowds strewn across its path. Gods, the flame-guy is fast. His blue light is now about twenty yards distant, parallel with the trampoline squad, and then he's past them, still heading our way.

"Emilia, mi querida hija," the man calls out. "And Gillian Halkey. Is that really you?"

"Dad?" Mel doesn't sound angry anymore. She sounds like that six-year-old who hid with me in the basement, the one who tried so hard to be brave.

"Damn it. For fuck's sake." There's a heaviness pushing down on my chest. Mr. Bareilles used to be so beautiful. Dead, he looks like a horror-movie skeleton or his old-bedroom shrine's Catrina statue minus her dress.

In the end, it's Becca who scurries forward to greet Mr. Bareilles while Mel and I do absolutely nothing.

The fourth rule states, *he must not behave in a normal manner toward his family*. Yet another law Mel and I have managed without even trying. No hugs. Not even a smile. Our reaction to Mr. Bareilles is not even close to normal. I guess it's huge Gilgamesh high fives all round.

"Mel, sweetheart, can't either of you ever just do as you're told? You're both way too early. I almost missed my new favorite activity: underworld bodyguard." Mr.

Bareilles has stopped less than five feet away. His flame-encased jaw moves as he talks, his right hand gesticulating, just as though his fingers were still covered by warm living flesh. Unbelievably, Mr. Bareilles, that crazy man, sounds almost happy. Skeleton or not, the guy is totally Mel's dad.

"What? Dad, how did you know? Did Becca tell you? I mean…Oh, Adala."

Now that he's so close, I can make out Adala, following in Mr. Bareille's spark-filled wake.

The green hues in Mr. Bareilles's fleshless grin flame higher. "Of course, Adala. Those girls aren't the only members of the Rampant's support staff. I'm thrilled to see you, mi querida hija. It's the most wonderful awful gift I've ever received, even better than that Rapture you're going to ignite."

In what has to be a first for the Plains, two dead girls, two living girls, and one parental skeleton stand in a cave, bickering over the best way to achieve the end of the living world.

"The faster we get you out of the Plains the better," Mr. Bareilles states for what seems like the millionth time. "Do you think you two can manage to steer something besides a canoe? It's like ancient times down here. Limited materials, limited tools, and no sense of hydrodynamics."

"What are you talking about, Dad?"

"The boats down here are all round. Our very own death-world special." Mr. Bareilles offers up his version of a dead-man's grin. His jaw slides down and back while each of his teeth become ringed in blueish-green flame. Surreal or not, for a moment everything feels just that little bit better; Mr. Bareilles's enthusiasm and his lame dad jokes have managed to find their way to the underworld.

"Dad, focus!" Mel says, just like we were all still back at home. "We're early, remember? We don't have a death-world special or anything else." She pauses and turns to me. "Do you think maybe we can we swim for it? We have the Rampant's protection on our side, right?"

"It's the Hubur River, Mel. It's a god-built underworld barrier."

"Okay, so no?"

"Pretty much."

And then Mel and I are grinning at each other. Team-work and lame Bareilles jokes all around.

"You and Mel are going to be just fine, mi querida hija." Even dead Mr. Bareilles's tone is so damn soothing. "How much work is left on that boat of yours, Adala?"

"Come, I will show you." And then he and Adala are wandering away from the cave's entrance to inspect the boat inside, leaving Becca with me and Mel.

"Hey, I haven't seen you two before," someone from the trampoline circle calls out.

"We should go inside," Mel mutters. She reaches for my injured shoulder, catches herself, and presses her hand against my lower back, urging me back into the green-lit cave.

Mr. Bareilles and Adala are bent over the rounded boat frame like they're inspecting some old car engine.

"A boat and safe passage. Both are needed. That has always been the issue," Adala says, looking at Mr. Bareilles with that strangely intense expression, though perhaps all corpse faces look that way.

"Agreed," Mr. Bareilles says. He turns toward Mel and me, leaning a bony forearm against one of the boat's leather-covered ribs. "Girls, you two weren't sup-posed to arrive until this particular task was complete," Mr. Bareilles's tone is all wrong. Oh, shit. It's his reading voice, the one he used when the storms got freakishly loud and he tried to distract us with some adventure tale. Today's story: Winnie the Pooh and Eeyore Build a Sailing Ship to the Outer Circles of Hell. I don't trust that tone one bit, and it's clear Mel doesn't either.

"Dad, exactly how are we going to get a boat?" she asks.

"I'm sure Adala and I can improvise."

Deathly efficient, Adala seems entirely unimpressed by Mr. Bareilles's parental enthusiasm. "Matías, this conversation is not solving the problem."

Mr. Bareilles nods his skull decisively and claps his hands together. His bones make a clacking sound like castanets. "It's settled. Same plan from my end. I'll handle the fliers. I'll just add a boat to our exchange."

"But—" It's Becca, and her face looks all sorts of worried.

"Rebecca, Mr. Bareilles is here to help." Adala says, still staring at Mel's dad, just as though she can read the expression on his glowing, picked-clean skull.

"Becca, I need you to stay with Mel and Gillian inside the cave. Can you do that for me?" Mel's dad sounds fine, relaxed even, but those dimming blue flames of his…

Oh, Mr. Bareilles, I definitely don't trust this conversation.

"Dad, I'm not letting you go anywhere." Mel reaches out and grabs Mr. Bareilles's shoulder, wrapping her arms around his glowing, bony body. And there goes our good job with rule number four: a demonstration of familial love is on full display. Good. I no longer give a ratty goddess's ass about Gilgamesh, Pastor Edwins, or the six supposed rules. This is Mel's dad, the guy she's been searching for bit-by-bit for the last two years. No way is he running off without us.

"Cariño, the fliers won't help unless they're properly motivated."

"But Daddy—Dad—fliers are super stupid."

"That's what I'm counting on. Emilia, you and Gillian need to trust me, all right?"

"I mean it, Emilia," Mr. Bareilles says after Mel's silence drags on.

"All right. I promise." Mel says, telling him exactly what he wants to hear. Still, she doesn't let go.

"Emilia, I know what's necessary." Turns out dead flame-dads are even stronger than living fathers. Somehow Mr. Bareilles slips from Mel's grasp and sprints out of the cave and left, toward a dark cloud of demi-god fliers and their constellation of tiny rainbow lights about a quarter mile off. Mel though, my Mel, she's moving too, following her father out into the Plains. Trying, anyway. Becca and Adala have grabbed both of her arms. "Damn it! Let. Go. Dad, wait! Stop! What are you going to do?"

"Quiet, Emilia," Adala's tone is fierce. "Those fliers are going to come right for you if they know you're here." As much as I dislike Adala, I know she has a point. We're out in the open, the only two pieces of living flesh in this entire world. But sometimes logic isn't the most important thing. Sometimes it isn't even on the list.

I dive into the mass of tugging arms and ghostly, desiccated limbs, the four of us an almost-silent, flailing tangle in the cave entrance. It's Mel and Gillian versus two very determined second graders, which isn't as easy as it sounds. Turns out, dead little girls are crazy strong.

Off to our left, I catch glimpses of Mr. Bareilles as he pauses and grabs something from the ground. "Have faith," he calls, and then his flaming body is moving again in the wrong direction, away from his only daughter and toward the cloud of fliers.

"Daddy." Mel's on her knees, watching her father, Becca and Adala's arms and legs wrapped around her, holding her tight.

"Mr. Bareilles," I echo. Why is he determined to break Mel's heart?

But Mr. Bareilles ignores us and sprints forward, dodging around a Plains-worth of bodies—piled bodies, walking bodies, partial bits of corpse that still manage to lurch and tumble. Thank gods for small favors, this world's bioluminescent light makes it impossible to view most of the vast mass of damned humanity.

Mr. Bareilles is yelling as he runs. He's already half-way to the cloud of fliers, but I can hear the words just fine. We all can. "Willing sacrifice," he cries over and over again. Oh, gods. Mr. Bareilles is already dead, but this is the King of Heaven and Earth's world. Things can always get worse.

The cloud of fliers have stopped their idle circling. They're banking toward Mr. Bareilles. Of course, they're interested in finding out what exactly this crazy skeleton man has to offer. A willing sacrifice, living or dead, is the most powerful of human offerings. At the very least it gives a god, or demi-god with abandonment issues, one incredible high. Supposedly, given the right circumstances, it can do so much more. Right now I really don't care.

"Willing sacrifice!" Mr. Bareilles howls again. That thing he picked up from the ground, turns out it's some poor soul's femur, a femur he's now waving with one of his own skeletal arms.

Mr. Bareilles always told Mel and me that the pending Rapture hadn't changed a thing, not really. Most living creatures, even gods, still tally the odds before they act. Mr. Bareilles, however, was never careful when it came to the people he loved. Dead or not, he's racing right at that crowd of immortal fliers, determined to help us. Even dead Mr. Bareilles is braver than that stupid shoe-wearing Gilgamesh.

As the cloud of fliers moves closer, I can make out far more than their shadow wings. Some fliers hold bouquets of glowing green mushrooms in their hands, while others are covered in red and blue glowing worms that undulate across their flight feathers and burrow into their down. Above in the living world, a tiding of magpie demi-gods is pretty much a doomsday scenario no human can survive. But here on the Plains, the dead continue to walk, or stand, or in some cases circle a happily screaming stretched-out trampoline corpse. Just like in my dream travels, the human residents of this place completely ignore the fliers gliding overhead. Underworld Basics 101: the unwilling dead just aren't that tasty. Lack of interest is its own protection.

"A barter. For a willing sacrifice," Mr. Bareilles calls to the tiding of magpie-gods now wheeling overhead.

"Dad. Don't." Mel twists against Becca and Adala's clinging limbs.

Mr. Bareilles turns in our direction. "Mel, I need you to do as Adala says."

"Daddy. Please—"

"This is for the best," Adala breaks in. *Indomitable* is right.

Those rainbow-light fliers, like their brothers on the surface, come in two basic types: some have human heads on massive bird bodies, while others are the more standard model, human body plus bird head. Either way they are all intent on the same land-bound object: Mel's dad.

"Uuuh. hhhh." Mel makes a sound I haven't heard since that day on the field, like all the air is being forced from her lungs, any chance of happiness gone, as well.

No one should have to deal with their father dying twice.

Mel's sounds: of course one of the fliers catches on—his human head covered in a tangle of salt-and-pepper down—breaks away from his siblings and continues toward our tiny cave. The demi-god's upper torso gleams with jet black feathers, bands of white plumage surrounding his dark wings. He may have a human head, but when the Magpie-man opens his human mouth, his screeches are those of a frenzied bird. I know what he's thinking: living flesh tastes so much better than bones, even when the bones are willing. Mostly, though, he's thinking it's been way too long.

If he reaches us—Well, it's not going to be good.

My worry seems contagious.

"Oh mein Gott," Adala says, and then Adala and Becca are in full retreat, attempting to drag Mel back to the cave. And Mel, well, she might not be walking, but she's not actively resisting either. Of course, I follow the trio to the mouth of the cave. They've got Mel.

Crisis upon crisis. Fuck this.

"I am no one's willing anything," I turn and yell out at this nightmare world. The Magpie-man actually seems to understand. He lands about thirty feet away, pauses, and glances back at the rest of his brothers. His face, his gods-damn human face, I know that expression: indecisive.

Meanwhile, recently passive Mel is twisting and thrashing as the dead girls try to drag her past the entrance and into the green-glowing cave.

"I will tear your beef-jerky body limb from limb. I'm not leaving him to die alone." Mouth open. Teeth exposed. Mel means it. She's not letting Mr. Bareilles out of her sight.

As the dead girls slip into the cave alone, our imminent winged visitor shifts from foot to foot, but doesn't step closer. Mel remains focused on her dad and the cloud of fliers that encircle him.

Mr. Bareilles swings that thighbone like a fly swatter as he negotiates. I guess it's his underworld substitute for a pointy umbrella.

Flier, Mr. Bareilles, runaway girls, everything seems to be slipping into chaos.

"Gods-damn it." I feel a prick against the crook of my elbow. Looking down, my heart rate spikes higher. Becca has returned and is pressing a shard of bone against my skin while Adala holds a rounded section of dried flesh, some kind of crude bowl, underneath, ready, it seems, to collect the bloody drops. "What the hell are you doing?" It feels like the witches scene from that Macbeth film Mr. Bareilles made us watch. I never liked that movie.

"Drinking the Hubur is no good for living people," Adala explains, which is absolutely no explanation at all. She grips my arm, keeping it steady over her bowl. "I am trying to help you, Gillian Halkey."

Before I have a chance to protest further, the bottom of the bowl is coated in my blood, and the two dead girls have disappeared back into the cave.

There's a screech, an overwhelming stench of stale sweat and decay, followed by a dust cloud rising. The magpie-man is stirring up the remains beneath his clawed feet as he walks in our direction. Decision made, I guess. And not in our favor.

Adala, we could do with that help right about now," I call.

"Almost done," Becca replies from somewhere inside the cave. I hear a clatter of bones followed by a muttered "damn it." Is our little Becca actually swearing?

"Mel." I reach out, feel the rigid muscles beneath her sweatshirt. Being held by her. Being anywhere but here… It's not supposed to be like this. "Mel, the flier. We need to go."

"No, we don't." She stands statue-still, refusing to look away from her dad. Mr. Bareilles's bone weapon seems surprisingly effective, or perhaps it's Mr. Bareilles's words. Either way, the demi-gods keep circling, instead of diving down and clawing him apart.

I tug on Mel's arm, the two of us stumbling as I force her body around until she's facing the solo flier heading our way. "Stop being such an idiot! You're going right into that guy's stomach if you're not fucking careful! Human steak tartare."

I've never seen Mel look so torn. "Adala. Becca. Some help, please." I'm not sure if I want them to fight the nearby flier or help me drag Mel inside.

Kkkk ka kkkk ka, the flier shrieks just as Adala emerges from the interior of the cave, carrying one of those dried-leather bowls. "This will keep the teufel away."

"Gillian, please you need to drink." Somehow Becca has slipped beside me, movements unnoticed. She's holding out a curved piece of leather identical to Adala's. Inside I can see a dark weirdly clotted pool of what must be my own blood. "You need to drink this," Becca presses, like I'm some little kid who needs to drink her medicine.

"You too, Emilia." I look over in time to see Adala's jaw shudder up and down in a rough movement that reminds me of a ventriloquist's dummy. Adala's distress, it seems, is reflected in the stiffening movements of her body.

"Gillian?" Mel is looking at Adala's bowl, not reaching for it, but not backing away. The bird man is less than twenty feet away. There's not time for explanations. Mel's still wearing my Colts hat. Of course she is. She's Emilia

Bareilles. Have faith, Mr. Bareilles said. As long as we're alive, there's hope. But that sentiment only holds true if we reach the Netherworld. "Drink it, Mel," I say.

"Shit. Not exactly my preferred method of getting closer to you." All the same, Mel drinks from the proffered bowl. And I do, too, gagging it down, bitter and thick.

"Damn it, Gillian, you taste awful. Gods, I so wish we'd kept the water."

"Or at least the Pabst," I reply.

She snorts with sudden laughter.

No matter what happens, Mel and I are in this together.

"I'll be back in a minute," Adala says.

Time without the sun and its shadows is harder to hold on to. For some unknown length of time Becca, Mel, and I stand together at the mouth of the cave, watching Mr. Bareilles and the circling fliers, while Adala and that other fluffy thing watch us from just a few feet away. Funny, funny fluffy thing. The creature's head keeps tilting to one side as though trying to puzzle something out. Up, down, up, down, swing your partner round and round and round.

Mel and I are still together, still in the lands of the dead, but everything else has changed.

"Gillian, touch my hair. Touch me. Pleash love."

Mel's voice is slurred. And that's not the only strangeness. There's a weird ringing in my ears that keeps getting louder. And then there's that smell. A stench that overpowers the dank and earthy cave behind us.

I reach out and grasp Mel's hand. Hey, diddle diddle. My heart, gods, my heart jumps over the moon. Time to run, sad dish, sad spoon.

"What?" Mel says, wrapping an arm around my shoulders and pulling me closer.

Did I say those words out loud?

Mel's face looks way too blurry. I lean forward until my nose is only inches from hers. Now I can see her just fine. Her beautiful known-forever face. "Run to the river. Grab an empty boat," I enunciate slowly. "You and me. Our lives. Our plan."

Mel frowns and shakes her head as though trying to dislodge a cloud of buzzing black flies. "What was in that blood?"

"You and me," I press. Why is her voice so echoey? Even the wingbeats of the moths flying above us and through the cave toward the flesh field seem to be on reverb. Rebecca and Adala and that third person—do I know his name?—Why are they staring at me and Mel? This is a private moment, for the gods' sake. Living girls in love.

"Gillian's right. You two need to get to the shore," Adala says.

Good, now she gets it, I'm the one in charge.

"Dad. So helpless," Mel says. Or maybe I'm the one who's talking—

"Matías has a plan," Adala replies. "Go." Mel's frowning, and so is the fluffy funny man. Seems like he doesn't agree.

"Go," Becca says. "Follow your plan."

"The plan. The plan. There is always a gods-damn just-makes-it-worse plan," Mel sounds so broken. Suddenly tears are running, racing, sprinting down her cheeks.

"Gods." And then Becca is grabbing my hand, and somehow, I'm out on the Plains, stumbling after her, carrying Mel's pack. My shoulders don't hurt at all. It's like a minor miracle.

I can't see her, but I know Mel is following with Adala. Adala is friends with Mr. Bareilles. Of course, Adala will keep Mel safe.

"Gods," I agree, nodding my head at Becca.

The King of Heaven and Earth is the worst. Instead of bare rock under my boots, it's bones and skin. Some of it even moves. I try to stop obsessing about one particular word, writhe, fail, and try again. Boots, not sandals: a totally good call. Mel was crying, the sad little spoon. I shouldn't be out here with Becca. The dish runs away with the spoon.

"Come on, Gillian." I must have stopped because Becca's tugging on my arm. I try to turn back toward the cave and trip instead, find myself sprawled on my back, Mel's backpack beneath me. There's a dull crunch. I try not to think about what that crushed thing might be, whether it felt any pain.

From my new perspective, I see that Adala and Mel are still standing in the cave entrance, that magpie flier blocking their way. The cave is much closer than I expected. Becca and I have barely made any progress across the Plains.

Magpie-man spreads his wings, open his mouth, and let out another deep and bird-like *kkkk ka kkkk ka*.

How could I have forgotten? The flier is standing in the cave entrance, right next to Mel, towering over her, in fact.

"Mine," the Magpie-man screeches, actually managing speech this time. He lunges forward, ready to grasp Mel with one of his upraised claws.

No, I try to call out and fail to do anything but grunt.

"Unwilling," Adala barks.

I watch as she pulls Mel forward, and then, thank gods, the two of them take their first steps onto the flesh soil of the Plains.

I need to—I want to—My legs tremble, my arms as well. I can't get up.

Meanwhile Magpie-man hops after them, his right claw outstretched. "Living food. Willing sacrifice," he whines. What an asshole.

"No. Unwilling," Adala sounds like she's talking to a misbehaving child, as though the power of her voice can actually push him away.

Gods damn it, you piece of baby-jerky. That is so not the plan. I'm supposed to be the one in charge, I try and fail to say.

But Adala isn't listening to my silent diatribe, she's talking instead. "The skeleton offers willing bones for the safe passage of living flesh.

"No bones. Two lives." The look on his face. Is that demi-god actually sulking?

Idiots. All of them. It would take just a few steps to reach the cave. My body, meanwhile, is determined to remain sprawled on the ground, unmoving.

"One willing skeleton," Adala counters, like it's a lesson she's determined to hammer into his birdbrained head. "The living cross unharmed." She pauses, finds her calm. "An exchange."

And suddenly I get it. This was the Rampant's plan all along, even if we'd arrived on time. It's so damn obvious now. Of course, those fliers would never have left us alone once Mel and I pushed off from shore. A willing sacrifice, though. The high of Mr. Bareilles's bones. That's an exchange any flier would take. And here was Mel's dad with his big Mr. Bareilles heart enthusiastically following the Rampant-sanctioned script.

Mel got it right. All these plans keep making things worse and worser still.

"Come on, Gillian," Becca whispers. The chill of her cool fingers digs through my sweatshirt all the way to the flesh of my upper arm.

"No," I whisper right back, hiss really. I'm furious. Plan update: Mel and I are bringing Mr. Bareilles along, throwing his damn skeleton into our boat. Maybe living flesh provides benefits to those nearby. Maybe we can bring the dead along when we cross. It's not like anyone, even the godly, knows all the facts. And trying is always better than doing nothing.

The Magpie-man obviously agrees. He spreads his wings again and aims his body at Mel and Adala. No way is this part of my plan.

"No, gods-damn it!" This time I manage to get the words out. For some reason, my voice sounds exactly like Mr. Bareilles's. How odd. When I glance toward the cloud of fliers, it turns out Mr. Bareilles is yelling as well.

"That man needs to calm down," the trampoline says with some irritation, his own screams momentarily on pause. "You too young lady. Some of us need to focus."

"Definitely," one of his glowing buddies agrees. Our life-and-death drama is interrupting their post-death fun.

Meanwhile, the boat negotiations have been forgotten, and Mr. Bareilles is sprinting back toward the cave, trailed by a swarm of fliers. His blue glow is a leaping, sparking blaze. "Hold on, Mel! Hold on."

"Darling, can you take this somewhere else? Pretty please?" one of trampoline's more mummified friends calls out. "We are trying to accomplish something here."

"Gillian, your blood is the worst." It's Mel

When I glance back toward the cave, I find her leaning against Adala's rigid body. Her blurred form no longer has a blue top. Instead, it's brown: Mel's hair. She's gods-damn lost my lucky Colts hat.

And then I'm not thinking about Mel or my hat or that stupid hungry bird. There's a sour-metallic taste in my mouth, and the ground when I look down seems to be slowly pulsing up and down. "Becca. Gods. What exactly did you guys give us?"

"Please, Gillian." Becca's voice sounds far too small. "Mr. Bareilles. He and Adala just knew you guys would never agree."

"Listen to me, your bird-godness. A true offering. A willing sacrifice," Mr. Bareilles bellows as he sprints forward, the rest of the fliers still following like a ragged feathered cloud.

"Will you all just shut up," declares the trampoline man. The rest of his troop have set him aside in favor of the new and unexpected spectacle. At least they made sure he had a view. His body is propped up like a mirror or picture frame with one of his ends stuck into the ground.

"Willing sacrifice," Mr. Bareilles repeats, ignoring the trampoline-man's complaints. Then I realize what's been bugging me. When he speaks, Mr. Bareilles doesn't even sound winded. Then again the guy doesn't breathe anymore.

"Not funny," I whisper to myself, not liking the glibness of the thought. "Cut it out."

"What did I say?" Becca looks confused.

"Nothing."

Both of us watch as, Mr. Bareilles stops near Mel and Adala, while the rest of the fliers settle a little farther off.

"Moveeee," something whispers from beneath me.

"Becca—"

"Moveeee," the same voice repeats, this time more emphatically.

"It's alive," I say, which is totally not true, but Becca gets my meaning.

"Don't worry," she says as she grasps me around the waist with her cold, glowy arms. "One. Two. And three. Easy peasey lemon squeezy."

Thank the gods, I'm finally upright again, though my legs seem uncertain about this new position.

"Gillian, don't come any closer," Mr. Bareilles calls out.

"Right." By which I mean that I wish I could.

"I am willing." Mr. Bareilles says, turning his attention back to the Magpie-man. He and Adala are really pushing that particular agenda, though I notice he's careful to keep out of claws' reach. "The bones of a willing sacrifice in return for safe passage."

"Crossing?" Magpie-man shifts from foot to foot, clearly unconvinced.

"Daddy, I feel ssssick." Which I'm willing to bet it's just a ruse to get him to back the hell off and cut out the sacrificial bullshit.

"Cariño." Mr. Bareilles says, then seems to run out of reassuring words.

"Hungry," shrieks the demi-god.

I know just what he's thinking: these birds are big feathered impulse machines, and there Mel is right in front of him, looking so damn tasty.

Mr. Bareilles frowns at the demi-god, seemingly working through some new thought, then his face clears, and he's waving his arms, a big enthusiastic target. "What you need, de dios, are my bones and *living* humans. Bits of the recently alive can't get you across the Hubur River."

Mr. Bareilles points toward a boat now pulling back toward shore after another failed demi-god attempt at crossing over. "A boat made of random bones and skin. Of course that didn't make it through to the Netherworld. But a journey with living humans, these specific living humans, and my parental bones. That is a journey filled with power."

I hear Becca's sudden inhalation. Oh man, even for Mr. Bareilles, this is some inspired piece of pseudo-logic.

"Daddy, whaaa…no." Sedated or not, even Mel knows this isn't good.

Mr. Bareilles ignores us all. His whole attention is on Magpie-man.

Meanwhile, Becca's plucking at my arm, trying to figure out what to do next. Problem time: I am too.

"Bones everywhere," another flier objects, stepping forward. Despite his beak and beady bird eyes, he speaks just fine. The rest of his brothers watch, a tiding of shifting restless discarded demi-gods.

"Yes," Mr. Bareilles agrees.

The second flier is now standing close enough to crush Mel's dad with his enormous half-godly beak.

"But I am a father. I love my girls. A father's love makes for one very special boat frame. These particular bones will follow their daughters all the way to the Netherworld."

Oh, Mr. Bareilles, you and your fucking insane heroics. Pretending to be my dad. Making sure Mel and I remain a package deal even now.

"Living flesh," the Magpie-man repeats, more quietly than before. He folds his wings back against his body, and looks toward Mr. Bareilles rather than Mel.

"Oooo, this is getting good," murmurs a man from the trampoline contingent. Their entire circle is clearly enthralled. All that's missing is the popcorn.

"God, the King of Heaven and Earth, loves his children deeply, just as I love mine," Mr. Bareilles presses, ignoring the sideline commentary. This is the big sell: the King of Heaven and Earth is their father. He supposedly loves them all. Sure it's bullshit. But it's also inspired. Even banished demi-gods yearn for their father's love.

The Magpie-man now stands less than a foot away from Mr. Bareilles. He could strike at any time. But his head is tilted to one side, as though he's more than halfway convinced. And he's not the only demi-god who feels this way. A few of the other fliers are nodding their heads as well. "Father's love" is clearly a powerful argument. It even sounds good to me. Perhaps it really does take a boat of bones willing to sacrifice everything to break through a godly barrier. Perhaps it really does take Mr. Bareilles's love.

"Bonessss," Magpie-man cries.

"Father Bonessss," the nearby bird-face responds.

And then, before Adala or anyone else has time to react, a flier with downy-chick hair breaks away from the crowd of demi-gods, grabs Adala by the shoulders, and takes off, heading toward the river's white-pebble shore. Adala doesn't struggle, and it's easy to figure out why. Even I know those talons could tear her dried little body apart.

Mel. Without Adala's hands to support her, she slumps toward the ground. Maw open, the bird-face and his naked human legs take a few steps in her direction. The high of living flesh: it seems he can't help himself.

"No." Mr. Bareilles's blue flame-head flares as he dives forward.

And he's not the only one.

God-like, Super-fucking-man like, Magpie-man is a blur I can't quite make out. Somehow, Mel is in his claws, and he's lifting her into the air, following the same trajectory as Adala and her downy-haired carrier toward the river. There's a rustle of feathers and displaced air as the rest of the King of Heaven and Earth's disinherited fliers follow. Turns out proof and commonsense are irrelevant when it comes to things like hope; the abandoned believe fiercest of all.

"Well, thanks gods, that's finally over," one of the trampoline crew says. "Ready, darling? One, two, three. Up you go. This time, Hubert, really put your back in to it."

The circle is once again ready to work. The human trampoline starts screaming. This time I can definitely sense the edge of happiness inside all that noise.

"Gillian, we need to go." Becca's trying to tug me toward the river, failing, at least until something bony and hard grips me around the waist.

"It's going to be all right," Mr. Bareilles murmurs, patting my shoulder with his de-fleshed hand. Of course he does. True or not, it's exactly the kind of thing he said when he was alive.

The demi-gods allow their father-love boat-framing-material—Mr. Bareilles—to make his own way to the river along with me and Becca. Maybe it's easier than arranging a ride down for all of us, or maybe it's something else entirely. Maybe they figure Mr. Bareilles won't go anywhere while they have Mel. That's what I'd figure, too.

"Gillian, you need to get across, fast, before they change their minds." Mr. Bareilles pauses, holds in whatever distracting feeling is punching up, a Rapture-trained survivor even now.

"Okay, Mr. Bareilles." Somehow there's got to be a way we can all be all right. My last shreds of hope push my legs toward the Hubur River, well that and Mr. Bareilles's love.

"We can take you with us. I just know we can." As I walk forward, I start to feel sick all over again.

"Gillian, shhh. It's going to be okay." If Mr. Bareilles had any flesh left, I'm sure he would give my hand a squeeze. As it is Mr. Bareilles settles for that bony hand on my shoulder. Bony or not, it feels good to have a parent with you in the land of the dead.

The Small Catechism
[of the Sumerian Revivalist Church]

To all faithful and upright pastors and preachers.
Grace, mercy, and peace in our God,
the King of Heaven and Earth,
and in all his godly and demi-godly children.

The Hubur River

Introduction

I have something to say to you! Heed! At the gate to the city of Ganzer, with the Hubur on all sides, both the godly and the broken wept.

Question: Who can cross from the Plains to the Netherworld?

Answer: Neither the imperfect dead nor the godly shall travel down the Hubur River and enter the Netherworld.

Routes to the Netherworld

1. Passages created at the beginning of time are open to the perfect dead. Each of these passages is guarded by the King's own godly children.

2. Utu the sun god, along with the sun, are granted entrance to the Netherworld each night.

3. Like Gilgamesh, all living who reach the Plains may cross the Hubur River and enter the final realm.

Those Who Shall Not Pass

1. The spoiled remains of the imperfect dead are forever relegated to the Plains.

2. Though the goddess Ereshkigal oversees the land of the perfect dead, the King of Heaven and Earth's other children shall never enter the Netherworld.

Question: Does the King of Heaven and Earth ever visit the dead?

Answer: The King of Heaven and Earth shall remain separated from the Netherworld for all of eternity.

Chapter 5

The keel of Enki's little boat was trembling as if it
were being butted by turtles, the waves at the bow
of the boat rose to devour the king like wolves and
the waves at the stern of the boat were attacking
Enki like a lion.

—from "Gilgamesh, Enkidu and the Nether World"

[*The Electronic Text Corpus of Sumerian Literature*,
Oxford University]

The Hubur River

Pastor Edwins used to call the Hubur River the Ocean of
Death. He was wrong. It's not an ocean. It's big, though.
The dried riverbed of the Ohio River down toward Lou-
isville is a tiny creek in comparison.

Adala, Becca, Mel, and I are sitting on the edge of the
shore in a hide-covered boat that has been pulled half-
way onto it. Nearby, the grounded cloud of demi-gods
separates us from the rest of the Plains and any hope of
escape. Our underworld faction of girl power has been
well and truly pressganged. Adala and Becca huddle in
the center of the boat, one of Adala's desiccated arms
slung across Becca's glowing shoulders, while Mel and I
straddle the skin-woven bench closer to the shore, keeping both the land and the dead girls in our line of sight.

"Don't worry," I tell Mel, but all I get in return is a
scowl. The girl is no fool.

Mel's backpack and a set of bone oars rest next to our feet. Listening to the bird chatter, it's clear why Adala and Becca have been added to our boat. The two dead girls are death detectors, a kind of early warning system just in case Mr. Bareilles's father-love thing doesn't work out. Though for the eternally trapped, they look pretty damn confident.

Besides our own boat, a second one rests a few feet away on the seemingly pebbly, yellow-white beach, but that's it.

"Not enough bones!" screams a bird-head when two of their number suggest adding more boats.

This narrow stretch of beach is Underworld Center. Up close, the truth is impossible to avoid: it doesn't contain a single stone. Along with the glowing click beetles and railroad worms that infest all things Plains, the shoreline is made up of teeth—pearlescent baby teeth, thick plaque-encrusted molars, incisors with their roots still intact—an untold lifetime's worth of teeth separated from their jaw-bone homes.

The fliers don't give a shit. "Flesh boat. Living Fleshhh," they repeat, nodding their heads and beaks importantly. Mr. Bareilles and his ideas have become their supposedly sure thing. The demi-gods just need to disarticulate one specific dead-and-doting father and attach his separated bones to the prow of the second boat, and then follow me and Mel, and our living flesh, into the Netherworld.

Idiots. If it wasn't so awful, it would be funny.

A couple of particularly muscle-y human-armed fliers—winged, Incredible Hulk types minus the green skin and emotive eyes—are busy modifying boat number two. I watch as they lash the leg bones of the unknown dead to the outer frame. Hallelujah and praise all gods. It's perches for everyone on this caravan ride to the Netherworld.

It wasn't supposed to go down like this. In all those Rampant dreams, never once did he mention sacrifice. That's the only thing I'm sure of as I sit in our boat waiting for whatever is going to happen next. Mel is sitting across from me, so close that our knees actually touch. Through the thick fabric of my jeans, I can feel the volcanic heat of her body. Damn Adala. Damn Mr. Bareilles as well. This should have been our moment, mine and Mel's. We're about to ride a boat away from this hell and into the perfect land. Now that sounds like a real first-love, end-of-the-world adventure. I force myself to push away the brushfire of anger and focus on the here and now.

"Mr. Bareilles, please." I turn my body until I'm facing the shore. "You can't do this, not for a second time."

"I need you girls to hold on just a bit longer, Gillian. It'll be over soon." Mr. Bareilles is standing next to the tiding of fliers who want to tear him apart, still trying to cheerlead us on. But underneath, I can feel his fear.

"Mr. Bareilles, this is bullshit. The fliers—"

"—shouldn't concern you. A boat is what you need, and here you are in a perfectly sturdy vessel."

"But—" Even for Mr. Bareilles, this is a whole new level of parental make-believe.

"Gillian, are you even listening? Soon the two of you are going to be safe." The man manages to sound parent-irritated even as the blue flames surrounding his body flare higher. He's definitely afraid.

Fucking parents. They're the absolute worst at prioritizing, even the good ones. Maybe especially the good ones, always trying to keep those monsters at bay. Thanks to Mr. Bareilles, my runaway heart has officially slipped into a new even-sadder gear. And then thank the gods, rage, that fear-purifying explosive, floods my brain. And I'm not the only one.

"Oh, I got it, Dad. I came all this way, and you're not even going to stick around. What kind of father puts his kid through his death twice?" Mel is yelling in that shrill high-pitched voice she gets when she's really upset. A couple of the closest fliers puff out their neck feathers, turn, and give me the stink-eye.

"That's just not true. Mel, you girls have always been the best of friends. And now, it seems like— Well, there's just no way you would have let Gillian wander down here alone."

"Mr. Bareilles, are you really trying to pin this mess on me?" There is no way I'm going to let that one slide.

"No, of course not. Sweethearts, can you both please just calm down?"

"Calm down?!" If he had any flesh left, I would strangle him dead. He's the one who should be yelling, hating on the world for all he's worth.

"Yes, Gillian, that would be nice. I'm not exactly looking forward to the next few minutes." I try not to notice how his voice trembles. Fail completely.

"Dad, I want to stay here with you."

"How?" I ask, though of course I mean "What about me?"

"You'd stay, as well. I just want us all to be together."

Oh man. Game, set, and match. My poor poor Mel.

I can feel Mel take a breath and find her way to those next words. "Dad, what's going to happen to you?

"I love you Mel, whether I'm alive, dead, or double-dead."

"What?" I seem to have lost the thread of our conversation.

Mr. Bareilles waves one of his skeletal arms, encompassing both the dead-eating river and the tooth-strewn shore. "It's not like the King of Heaven and Earth has bothered to come up with a better phrase for what happens down here. Too busy fretting over his messy house and the fact that all his Rapture servants are incredibly late for work." And then the fucker, the fucker who is breaking both our hearts into so many little-girl pieces, actually has the nerve to laugh, a supposed dad joke that fails so damn hard.

And Mel, she actually stirs at the sound of his laughter, sits up, leans her head against my shoulder. "Dad, such a stupid joke."

I reach over and stroke Mel's hair, smile despite myself. But the moment doesn't last.

Kkkk ka kkkk ka. The cry rolls through the tiding of fliers. Attention, attention, attention, the sounds seems to say. This de-boning meeting is called to order. Time for the real show to begin.

Love finds a way. Despite the blood sedative, and her dad's words of warning, Mel attempts to rise, but I turn and lock my arms around her, holding her still. Adala and Becca got that part exactly right: girls should not be sacrificed, even by themselves. Mel letting herself get hurt, Mel letting herself get killed. No. Not on my watch.

Back on the shore Magpie-man, the bird-brain nominally in charge, steps toward Mr. Bareilles while the rest of the fliers form a loose circle around the two of them, all legs and feet and claws. Through the gaps, I can see Mr. Bareilles in the center.

At some signal I don't quite catch, a second flier—human bodied, bird headed—steps inside the circle. Beaker Slicer, some corner of my brain silently anoints him. Damn that stupid parent-man. Mr. Bareilles isn't even taking a defensive stance.

"Gillian, take care of our girl." Mr. Bareilles says, the same words he repeated every time Mel and I pushed off in that old green canoe we used for our Farrigan River adventures.

Our girl. Our Mel.

"Dad."

"I'm here, Mel, right here."

I tighten my arms around her as we both look out toward the shore.

Mr. Bareilles is nothing but fire-encased bones. There are no ligaments holding together his skeletal form. Doesn't matter. I can *see* Mr. Bareilles. I can feel the expression on his face. He glows blue-flame fiery with love for Mel, and for me, as well. Mr. Bareilles is the best dad I never had. No matter what happens, I'm so glad we found him.

"Nooo." Mel says as I cradle her close.

Beak Slicer chooses this moment to make his move, grasping Mr. Bareilles's shoulders with both of his human hands and opening his beak wide. Mr. Bareilles, our Mr. Bareilles, doesn't even flinch.

Crack. There's an audible snap as the first of Mr. Bareilles's ribs pulls free.

I feel the boat rock slightly. I hear Becca's half-stifled gasp.

"Shh, little one," Adala whispers.

Mel's biting into my arm, not crying out, working so hard to stay silent.

"What a gods' awful world," I grind out, and I don't mean the pain.

"It's all right, Gillian, Emilia." Mr. Bareilles is trying so hard, smiling in our direction with all his gumless might. "It doesn't hurt. Cariño, Emilia, please, do me one last favor."

"Dad…"

"Please, girls, I need you to look away."

I hear Becca start to cry.

"You, too, Rebecca Chavis. Got it?" Mr. Bareilles sounds stern, like he's going to tell our mothers if we don't get our acts together and do as he says.

"Yes," Becca replies, her voice low. "Mr. Bareilles, I'm so sorry."

"None of that, Rebecca. It's all right."

Why do I keep getting it all so wrong? This journey was supposed to end in happily ever after. I swing my left leg over the bench and turn away from the shore, making sure Mel does the same. Adala and Becca. I thought I'd be incandescent with fury at their colossal stupidity. I'm not. The two of them are huddled together on the center bench, a couple of dead little girls trying to avoid the merest splash of water. Even in death, there is so much to fear.

Meanwhile, Mel has wrapped her arms around her bent knees. She's one moment away from rocking back and forth, one thought away from screaming.

"So I guess I'm the designated rower," I say, sighing. Did I imagine it, or did Mr. Bareilles just laugh at my lack of enthusiasm? It would be just like him to catch that one last joke. He used to call me "the Halkey's designated reluctant rower." And it's true. Out on the Farrigan River, I usually let Mel do most of the work.

Our assigned boat looks the same as all the other underworld boats. It reminds me of one of those Tibetan coracles Mr. Bareilles talked about during one of his boat-building crazes. It's roundish and unwieldy like a ten-foot-long, halved walnut shell. The way Mel's dad explained it, before fiberglass and planks of wood, people used whatever was on hand, reeds and branches they bent into boat frames. Without access to manufacturing or lengths of wood, down here the gods do the same thing. The key difference: their building materials are human bones.

"Adala—was sacrificing Mr. Bareilles really the Rampant's gods-damn plan?" I try to keep my eyes on the two girls. Still, I can't help noticing the flurry of movement off to the side as the two Hulk-arms lash the first of Mr. Bareilles bones to the bow of the second boat. Why is everyone so willing to sacrifice themselves—and each other—to help us reach the Netherworld? The Rapture doesn't even remotely seem worth all this pain.

"Do you know how I ended up down here?" Adala says, seemingly trying to change the subject.

"No." My voice is not encouraging.

"On my last day, the bricklayer gave me a shiny, red apple," Adala continues, ignoring my tone. Her eyes track the activity behind me as she talks. Her dried-up face is almost entirely immobile, making it impossible to read her reaction.

Crack.

Mel flinches, her arms dropping from her knees as she starts to turn.

"You promised," Mr. Bareilles barks.

Which of course we didn't. Still, Mel keeps her back to the shore, arms wrapped around her knees once again as I focus on Adala. Her face bothers me far less than before. "Apples?" I prompt. "And bricks?" Listening to Adala's story has got to be better than waiting for the next sound.

"Ja. The bricklayer gave me an apple to keep me quiet while he worked. I loved apples. My mother stood and watched, holding the purse of coins the man had given her while I stepped inside the bridge's wall. Do you know what they said when I tried to get up from that wooden stool? 'Your sacrifice will keep the bridge strong.' Later, once the bricklayer's work was done, it was dark—and cold. And I was so, so thirsty."

"Girls shouldn't be sacrificed," Becca says, echoing her earlier words. She squeezes Adala's dry little hand.

"No, Becca, they shouldn't." I agree. "And neither should Mr. Bareilles." I mean it. No matter how it turns out, hurting others isn't supposed to be the goal.

There's another *crack* from the shore.

I can feel Mel's trembling body pressing into mine.

"We tried to think of a way to save Mr. Bareilles." Becca's little-girl face looks completely overwhelmed as she gazes down at her hands, her lap, anywhere but directly at me and Mel. "We didn't want either of you stuck here like us. But Mr. Bareilles, he said we had to choose. It was so hard…" Her voice trails off. That little holographic face. She looks like she's about to cry.

"Becca—" I pause. I'm the one who left her behind on our walk to school. And what about Adala? How long did she have to wait, bricked-in and alone before landing here in the underworld? Adala was buried alive to ensure a stone bridge, an inanimate object, never fell. The Rampant's plan is no different, full of human sacrifice and epically fundamentally wrong.

And once again it's people, loyal good-intentioned people, who have brought it to fruition.

There's another snapping sound, followed by a clacking, like the rough shaking of bones. I can't help myself; I turn and look over my shoulder toward the shore.

One of the fliers is passing a rib and some smaller bones—maybe fingers? maybe toes?—to the fliers working on the second boat.

"Gillian Louise Halkey," Mr. Bareilles calls. "You have one job, steer that boat through. Emilia, leaving this place, that's the important thing."

Mel turns and stares at her father. The last of Mr. Bareilles's bone body is strung between the magpie-man's wings as Beak Slicer reaches for yet another piece. I can see Mr. Bareilles's spinal column and skull along with one arm, but there's not much else. "We could've found another way."

"No."

"You didn't even let us try."

"Honey, don't. This place—Just a few years down here, and I've done things… At least that's over."

"Whatever you did, you shouldn't have to be perfect," I say, unable to hold back the words. All this judgment falling down, crushing both the living and the dead. The King of Heaven and Earth, this whole place: It's one giant setup and it's always the people who lose.

"Gillian, Emilia, please. I need you to make it through." Mr. Bareilles pauses for a moment. "I'm just so glad I got to see you girls one last time. I'm so proud of who you've become." He sounds tired. But his blue-flame still glows steady and bright. "You know, double-dying doesn't hurt nearly as much as that first kind."

"Mr. Bareilles, what will…" I don't know how to complete the sentence. Does the Mr. Bareilles part of Mr. Bareilles really just disappear once all his bones are torn apart?

"Only one thing I know for certain," he replies. "I won't be able to get up early to take you girls to school. Or fill that damn generator with gas. No different from single-dying, I guess." His face might not show anything, but I can tell he's laughing, just a little bit. "You know, that part of double-dying isn't half bad. At least there's no more work." Mr. Bareilles. I already miss him so much.

Mr. Bareilles. At this point all that's left is a collection of smaller bones—phalanges, vertebra, sesamoids—and his head. The fliers are picking through the pile, looking for just the right length to fill those last empty slots on their special boat.

"Careful," Magpie-man screeches. Two of the flock are tussling, kicking up the remaining bones as they tug at Mr. Bareilles's skull and try to pry off his jaw. Despite Magpie-man's warning, Mr. Bareilles's remaining hand slips and falls into the shallows.

I bend toward the water and watch as Mr. Bareilles's fingers finally separate, the joint of each bone released from its companion. The separated bones sink into the river-gloom, while their glow sputters from blue, to murky yellow, until the light finally disappears.

"Cariño, I think I've finally got the perfect epitaph for my gravestone."

"Yeah?"

"He always had a flair for the dramatic, especially at the end. Get it?"

"Such a stupid joke…"

"Crossing," caws the downy-head flier. His fuzz-feathered face is only inches away as he leans in to check on Mel. How much temptation can one discarded demi-god take?

"Go," the remains of Mr. Bareilles whisper from the shore. "Please, you need to go."

"Go," Magpie-man agrees.

The fuzz-face exhales sharply, as though momentarily disappointed, and then pushes against the edge of our boat. And just like that, the four of us are out on the river: Adala, Becca, me, and Mel. The boat sways from side to side as the current begins to tug us forward.

"Remember to steer," Mr. Bareilles calls. "Gillian, you need to use those oars." Dead people are so confusing. I have no idea how he can even see us.

I reach for both oars, set their bone handles against either side of the leather-clad boat, and then ease our coracle around until I'm facing the shore and the stern of our boat, along with Becca and Adala, is facing toward whatever lies ahead.

Meanwhile Mel has slipped off the bench and is sitting atop her backpack on the bottom of the boat. "It's a good thing I love you," I mutter, "because you, Emilia Bareilles, are one reluctant rower." I wish she would fire up and give me even the smallest bit of shit. Instead, she attempts a smile, fails, tries again. That smile of hers, it fucking breaks my heart. "Time to go." I plant my boots against the curving ribs that frame the bottom of the boat and begin to row, watching the shore recede behind us.

We're in the endgame now.

"This is going to work, Gillian," Adala says, just as though this has always been the plan: she and Becca riding the Hubur River to the Netherworld, or oblivion, whichever comes first.

I adjust my grip on the rounded joint of the oars' bone handles and pull, ignoring the ache in my shoulders. Mel, Mr. Bareilles, and I used to sneak down to the Farrigan River before it dried out completely. People weren't supposed to navigate those waters either. We are going to do this. After all the sacrifices, Mel and I are going to make it through.

"Follow," a bird-man croaks. I watch as that tiding of fliers jockey for position on their own boat's bone perches. The tiding contains about thirty fliers. It's obvious their coracle can't carry them all. Almost a dozen runts are forced by their brothers to take to the air, circling close to the boat and Mr. Bareilles's disarticulated bones.

Out on the Farrigan, Mr. Bareilles always offered us a sip from his special stash of Pabst Blue Ribbon. "The two of you are better than those gods any day of the week," he'd say, before handing over the can.

I can feel the sweat sliding down my back and along my arms. Even with the drugged blood Adala and Becca fed me, the pain is starting to bleed through. Meanwhile, my drainage pipe injuries are making their needs clear. Their loudest demand, the one I continue to ignore: no more rowing.

"Going," a flier calls as the second boat slips into the river, Magpie-man at the prow and the overhead cloud of demi-god runts sticking close. There's a smack of bone on water as Magpie-man tosses something round and hollow into the water. I wish I didn't know what it is: Mr. Bareilles's skull.

"At rest." The words rise from the water, an unexpected gift that quickly fades, along with Mr. Bareilles's faint blue glow. After that it's just the splash of our oars and those of the second boat, accompanied by the flapping of flier wings and snapping beaks. Mel sits behind Adala and Becca, all of them facing me and whatever the river reveals. Mel's expression seems frozen. Beyond the stern of our boat, I see the second boat about twenty feet away. It rides low to the water; even with the added perches, the weight is way too much. The boat is meant to hold ten fliers tops, and that's if the birds all work together, wings held in tight.

Meanwhile, in the bioluminescent glow generated by the underworld's algae, fungi, and insects, the shadow-wings of the Rampant's moths and magpies continue to stream above us, heading toward the cave and their specially prepared flesh field.

"I don't get it." I eye the second boat, the crowd wheeling overhead, before returning to Adala and Becca. The truth surrounds us. I can't be the only one who sees it. "You guys, how can you be so calm? You have to know there's no way—" I stop as Becca turns and huddles into Adala's shoulder.

Of course they know. Plenty of underworld bones, both godly and human, were driven to attempt this journey. None of them made it.

The real truth: Becca, our Becca, is traveling a river whose waters will destroy her, on a boat that won't allow her to reach the safety of the Rampant's domain. Adala, as well.

"You wanted to ask a question?" Adala is looking directly at me as she cradles the younger girl, daring me to say it out loud, hoping I won't.

Taking care of Becca until the end. That's what I should be focusing on.

I shake my head. "Soon," I say, instead. "We'll get there soon."

"There's always an end, Gillian Halkey," Adala says. "And sometimes you can't stop it even when you know it's coming. I was telling the truth earlier. I really do believe girls should stick together, especially at the end."

Becca presses even harder against Adala, the only sign that she's aware of how truly bad things have become.

"Me too." I clench my teeth, ignore the pain in my shoulders, keep rowing. Their inclusion on this particular excursion wasn't my idea, and Adala and Becca aren't making a single move to stop me from rowing. I have never felt so complicit. I can't get my head around how much of this is my fault.

"Gillian," Becca whispers. "Don't be mad. Not now." She sounds so sad.

"Why did you let Mr. Bareilles agree to all this? Is that the act of a friend, Becca?" How can I be raging at this little girl? the part of me that isn't terrified and guilty and all things fucked-up asks.

"Friends also shouldn't leave little girls alone outside." Becca says from the cover of Adala's embrace. She's sparking with sudden indignation. "You left me all alone, Gillian. You and Mel both did." She raises her head and looks directly at me. "It hurt. A lot."

Her words are a fucking punch to the gut. "Becca, I didn't mean to—" I pause, the crutch of my anger destroyed. "Becca, you didn't deserve—Gods. I wish I could take it back. All of it. Everything I did that day. Everything that happened to you."

"Me too," she says, echoing my words of moments before. Even without the moisture of actual tears, it's clear she's crying. "Gillian, you have to believe me. It was the only way. Adala and I are trying to help you."

"I know," I say, meaning it. Mr. Bareilles's fucked-up logic makes a sort of sense: the few for the many and all that. He just didn't expect Becca and Adala to get caught up in the same trap. And my own choice to row this boat forward? It's an ugly-as-shit compromise. Sure Mel wins, but both of these girls lose.

Becca face is no longer scrunched up and weepy. I'm so glad she's not crying anymore. "I really wish life and death weren't so messed up," she says.

"Yeah." I take a steadying breath and continue rowing.

I glance over my shoulder, checking I'm still navigating toward the unknown. Less than a hundred yards away a rocky outcrop cuts off our view of whatever lies beyond. Just before the rocks, a tributary snakes off to the left. Even if the ceiling of this land weren't gradually sloping down and the stone walls weren't closing in just beyond the shore, the light of the algae blooms is becoming scarcer along with the glowing insect life. The Netherworld was close. Abandoned coracles bump against each other along the side channel, herded by some unforgiving eddy. A severed wing trails from the side of one of the craft, the tattered remnant of a downed flier. A number of boats are still burdened with their lost passengers' provisions: rope, oars, hide bundles of various shapes and sizes.

The only thing that could make this boneyard warning more clear is if the King of Heaven and Earth came down and announced it himself: only the living and the ungodly shall pass this point.

I focus on the oars: back and up, back and up. This is my only job right now. The second boat is only about ten yards back, the rower pulling hard while the smaller demi-gods continue to bank overhead. Mr. Bareilles is the P.T. fucking Barnum of the underworld. Those desperate birds are all in, pushing forward to the Netherworld no matter what commonsense and the river's own detritus should tell them.

The girls have no such illusion.

"It's too dark, Gillian. It's not supposed to feel so dark." Becca says. Adala blinks rapidly—SOS, SOS, we're tripping, falling, plummeting off the edge—tightens her arms around her friend. "Shh," she croons, swaying in time with the movement of my oars.

"We need to turn around," Mel murmurs. She's still looking back toward the second boat and the shore.

"No," Adala responds.

Gods.

The river narrows quickly after we pass beyond the outcrop, while the underworld ceiling continues to slope down. The shore has become a narrow strip of bone-and-tooth-pebbled land beyond which rests impenetrable stone. It no longer feels like we're on a river rushing across open land. There's no mistaking the tunnel closing in around us. What really disturbs me, though, is the loss of life. There are no more glowing insects and illuminated mushrooms. The prettiest of pretties, the water's bioluminescent algae, no longer surrounds our boat. We've come to the end. Our final crossing into the Netherworld is about to begin.

Even the fliers recognize the change.

"Flesh children," screams a flier perched on what looks to be one of Mr. Bareilles's ribs.

"Father bonesssss," cries another flier circling overhead.

To judge by the agitated tones, the demi-gods' doubts are escalating. Really, after all those flying assholes have gotten away with, how could they ever have equated parental love with unassailable protection?

I pull against the oars, bending and straightening my arms, as Magpie-man claws his way to the prow of the second boat. He seems determined to claim the closest position.

"Adala…" If Becca could press any harder against Adala, she totally would. As it is, she looks like she's trying to merge her fleshless body with Adala's hardened frame.

"You know." Mel pauses, then rallies. "You know, Gillian, this isn't exactly the romantic boat ride I was hoping for. Though, my sweet Becca, I really appreciate your excellent mood lighting."

And then miracle of miracles, Becca lets loose with an actual laugh. Mel, gods, she's a fucking rock star. She is my one and only light. Well, almost.

Mel wasn't lying. It's the literal truth, at this point our only light source is Becca and her glowing little-girl body. In the dim Becca-light I can see the second boat closing in. The *Clap-clap, clap-clap-clap* of Mr. Bareilles's smallest bones tapping against the hull of the fliers' boat sounds like Morse code for hurry, hurry, hurry. Despite his double-death, maybe somewhere Mr. Bareilles is still aware.

It's a comforting thought, anyway.

"Not working," hisses one of the runts from somewhere overhead. I follow its silhouette as it banks toward the overcrowded second boat and attempts to find a perch. At this point the cave's ceiling is barely high enough to allow for flight. If the air-bound fliers don't turn and retreat, they're going to end up in the de-articulating water.

kkkk ka kkkk ka,, Magpie-man cries, puffing out his chest and spreading his wings in agitation. The river carries the sharp clack of keratin beaks and claws as two more fliers clash over another one of Mr. Bareilles's bone perches.

I can feel the stone walls closing in. Soon I'll be able to reach up and touch the ceiling. Bird fucking brains. Once that happens there'll be no more flight, no more chance of demi-god escape. No boat is going transport them to the Netherworld and there is no way they can steer that crowded bone-and-leather boat against the current and back toward the Plains' toothy shore.

Powder-keg moment.

A hot breeze rises out of the darkness and forces itself against my face and hair. I send a prayer, or perhaps a wish, up toward the heavens as I push down on the oars. Please let there be a way through for all four of us. Becca and Adala aren't the only ones who are sick of girls being sacrificed.

"Gillian," Becca gasps as her spirit flesh starts to flicker like a TV screen just before the power goes out. Only that still-physical jaw bone of hers and the hanging bit of dried flesh remain steady and unchanged.

It's like a stop-motion sequence of still images: Magpie-man launching himself from the bow, spreading his wings, aiming his outstretched claws toward the stern of our girl-filled boat.

And then I'm sliding down, tumbling as our shell tips backward and the rock walls echo with a boat's-worth of cawing, raging man-birds. Somehow, I'm pressed against Mel, sliding toward the stern, Becca's cold little body on Mel's other side. No oars. No candles. No beer. No weapons left but my own human self.

"No. No. No." It's Mel. Rivulets of river water have started to lap over the sides of our coracle.

There's a smell of unkempt feathers and an acrid scent, like burning plastic, chemical and wrong as Magpie-man attempts to settle himself on the back edge of our boat. "All fathers be damned," he screeches. It's official. It's every magpie for himself.

"Away. Away." Adala snarls as she pushes Becca behind her toward Mel and the relative safety of the center of the boat. For a moment, the bird-man teeters and it almost seems as though the power of Adala's voice will actually force him back, but then Magpie-man steadies himself and Adala swings out with one of her desiccated arms, determined, it seems, to punch a ten-foot-tall demi-god.

Magpie-man twists his body to the side, and she misses.

The boat rocks even harder, starts to spin, and then a wave's worth of water splashes upward and over. That's all it takes. Just like that, half of Adala's arm is gone, river-eaten.

I'm soaked. Mel's soaked. Becca is kneeling on top of Mel's splayed out body in the middle of the boat, trying to avoid the rising puddle. In Becca's place, I'd be doing exactly the same thing.

"Adala." Her face, her voice—the girl is absolutely horrified.

"Becca, it is going to be all right." Adala's voice sounds almost gentle. "The two of us, we will stay together, I promise."

"But—your arm. The river."

"There is no pain," Adala says, though judging by her expression, I'm not sure that's entirely true.

"Are you serious?!" Is that me screaming? Suddenly, I'm the tiny bomb-face of the underworld. My heart feels like it's about to explode. "After everything you've been through, you're really going to let this happen?"

Puffs of steam are rising from Becca's lower body. Even with Mel as a riser, there's just no way to protect her body. Everything is wet: Mel, the backpack, the leathery cloth that makes up our boat. Meanwhile, Becca's glow continues to stutter: on, off, on, off. "Mr. Bareilles would be proud of us," Becca says with some indignation. "We're not 'letting this happen.' We're helping Mel live."

"And also killing some of the teufel," Adala adds with sudden vengeful glee.

Magpie-man is done with our pointless human talking. "Living flesh," he screeches from his perch on our stern. Still alive, with only some of us consumed, perhaps he can make it through, at least that seems to be his reasoning.

Magpie-man lunges past Adala and toward Becca and Mel, while I dive toward his sticking, feathery body. The two of us collide just to the aft of Mel. I hear the scrambling of multiple bodies as Becca and Adala move closer to the bow, Mel attempting to place her body between them and the demi-god currently invading our boat. And then there's a press of oily feathers against my nose, more filling my mouth. I'm down, pinned beneath the magpie, screaming as the boat pitches violently from side to side.

River water rises around me. My screams just won't stop. I don't want them to. I'm just so sick of holding everything in.

"Gillian." Becca. Her voice sounds so far away.

"It will be all right, liebling."

I know that tone. This is for the best, is what Adala really means. There is no heaven. We all know that. But at least Mr. Bareilles is at peace. Compared to this place, perhaps peace really is heaven. Who would understand that better than a centuries-old, dead, little girl?

"Gillian," Becca repeats.

Becca's still here, still present, even as the boat swamps and Magpie-man clings to my living flesh with all his might, trying to avoid the rising water.

I want to run. I want to fly up and away. I want to wake up in my bed and realize it's just another Rampant dream. Instead, I press my whole river-sodden self up against that magpie, legs to crown. That's when the Magpie-man adds his own voice to the cacophony. He's screeching, convulsing, scrambling to get away.

The fucker. I'm glad it burns.

I have just enough time to twist into a crouching position while the demi-god finds another perch. He's thrashing, balanced precariously on top of Mel's backpack. His claws look shredded, the nails gone. I hope it hurts like flier-hell.

It's then that the miracle happens. Becca's still in the boat, what's left of her anyway. She's sitting with Adala, the last of her body settled on the puddle-filled bottom, more cloud than human shaped. "I feel so good," she says.

"At rest," the waters murmur.

And then she's gone. Not with a whimper or a cry, but with a small smile, like that of a fevered child finally falling into sleep.

"Mel—" I start. "Adala—" trying to figure out what I want to say next. The boat however is still not at rest. Instead, the rocking is intensifying, powered by the Magpie-man's frantic movements. He's beating his wings, wafting the scent of rancid feathers right at me, Mel, and Adala as he tries to balance himself atop Mel's stupid, totally useless backpack.

"Girls shouldn't be sacrificed. Girls, you gods-be-damned bird, should be left in peace," Adala screams. She hurls herself past me and straight toward the stern. And then she's on him, grappling with Magpie-man, gripping his waist with both legs. Her ancient teeth tear into his neck as the dead-girl fingers of her remaining hand aim for his eyes. The demi-god doesn't stand a chance. He's too terrified of the water.

No more hesitation. "Girls should stick together," I howl, launching myself, injured shoulders first, against the tangle of demi-god and girl.

"Fuck this shit," Mel cries following close behind.

Adala: the nearby water, Mel and my wet living bodies, and the violent demi-god, none of it seems to matter.

"The water, Gillian. Get him in the wasser." Adala's little eyelids blink rapidly in time with her now stuttering light. And then all her attention is on Magpie-man as she batters her own hardened-flesh against his human skull. No sweat. No heavy breathing. Death has very few benefits, but this is one of them.

I grip Magpie-man's wings and try to hang on as I butt my head up against his jaw. His feathers feel as slippery as melting plastic. Meanwhile, Adala's still swinging. But he just won't fall. I shift my head forward, searching for a second target—his ears, his mouth, anything soft.

A bird-part smashes above my left eye, and the blood starts flowing. My hands seem to let go of their own accord. I'm sliding, falling back into the bottom of the boat as the injured demi-god sways, his claws bubbling and his balance almost gone.

"Now, Gillian Halkey!" Adala cries.

Fuck the pain. I barrel forward one last time, a full-body slam that tips the flier over the side and into the water. And Adala, her legs still wrapped around his waist, goes over as well. I cling to boat's bone frame while Mel grabs me from behind.

My eyes are covered in blood, and I'm crying. Sobbing, in fact.

Girls shouldn't be sacrificed. Not once. Not twice. Not after hundreds of years of hell.

The river is pulling hard, drawing the boat forward. I can feel the hot dry air swirling through the darkness. The flickering lights of Adala and Magpie-man are like sinking flares. There seems to be no bottom to the river as their lights go down, down, down. And then they're gone, both of them dying one last time.

Mel and I crawl toward the bow and wrap our arms around each other. Ahead of us is nothing but deepening shades of black. The blood on my face is the warmest thing left, that and Mel. After all those years of Camp Hallelujah, all those sermons discussing the tunnel of light, the Ascension, my crossing into the arms of God, I never imagined I'd willingly travel into darkness with only Mel by my side.

The last thing I notice is the fluttering of thousands of tiny wings. Somewhere above us the Rampant's moths and those baby-transformed magpies continue to stream through to the Plains and the flesh field beyond, intent on their own Rampant-fueled mission.

The Small Catechism
[of the Sumerian Revivalist Church]

To all faithful and upright pastors and preachers.
Grace, mercy, and peace in our God, the King of
Heaven and Earth,
and in all his godly and demi-godly children.

Judgment

Question: Will those who enter the Netherworld live in happiness once their journey is complete?

Answer: God, the King of Heaven and Earth does not tell us.

Chapter 6

In my city people are dying, and hearts are full of distress. People are lost... I craned my neck over the city wall: corpses in the water make the river almost overflow... No one is tall enough to reach heaven.

  —from "Gilgamesh and Huwawa"

[*The Electronic Text Corpus of Sumerian Literature*, Oxford University]

The Netherworld

"Hosanna and praise be," I say. The good news: we've made it. The almost-as-good: even in the Netherworld, irony is never out of style.

Mel is sitting on the bottom of the boat, leaning against one of the coracle's benches, while I'm sprawled on top of her, my head against her chest, my left arm flung across her soaking body. We managed the dark river crossing in this exact position, me gripping Mel as the coracle twisted and the water surged, battering the sides of the boat. Somehow, I never once let go. It's as though I believed sheer force of will—my will—would keep Mel from tumbling out, which, actually, I kind of did.

There are no more raging waters. From my prone position, I can see that our coracle is lodged in the shallows of a small cove under a seemingly endless sky. This place is nothing like the river world we left behind. There is no beach of human teeth or seaweed scraps of hair and bone. Even the glowing insects and fungi are gone, not that we need their light. The Netherworld sky glows a strange pearlescent gray. Daytime then, the god Utu and the sun haven't completed their nightly trek down.

This is supposed to be it: the moment when Mel and I ride with the Rampant back to Decatur, Indiana, and kick off the Rapture. Instead, my stomach feels like it's about to heave, while my shoulders and arms just want to curl up and die. Most telling, our boat's leather covering is full of tears and gouges. The boat is rapidly taking on water. It's as likely to survive a return voyage as me and Mel, which is to say not at all.

"You awake?" Mel asks. She sounds calmer than I expected. Tired, though.

"Yeah." Mel's chest rises and falls beneath me, her heart beating against my cheek. "Not dead yet," I say, reaching for the right words, failing. I have no idea what to say to this girl, this woman, that I love. That I have always loved. None of this journey has gone as planned.

One positive: here in the Netherworld, there are no more fliers. Just like every other realm created by the King of Heaven and Earth, the Netherworld was formed with its own invariable laws. With the exception of the goddess Ereshkigal, who is required to oversee the dead, and her younger brother Utu, who must visit the Netherworld each and every earthly night, this place is god and demi-god free.

Like the Law of Gravity in our living world, and the damned-forever law of the Plains, the foundational laws of the Netherworld are unchangeable. Not even the King of Heaven and Earth can enter these lands. The fucker.

"Mel, babe, we got things to do." I set my hands against the waterlogged bottom of the boat and raise my head. Mel's shirt pulls upward for a moment, my coagulated blood bonding cotton to flesh. Timing. This is not the way I want to undress her, and gods, it's definitely not the place.

"Babe? Really? That's what you're going to lead with?"

"Something like that…Babe." And then I'm sitting next to Mel, my ass resting in a puddle. Jeans were maybe not the best choice after all. Nylon and waterproof would have at least kept us dry.

With a bit of space between us, I can see Mel more clearly. Her heart might sound steady, but her skin is ashy, and her lips are bluish and all sorts of cold. "Gods damn it, Mel. I'm supposed to be taking care of you. You're freezing to death." Definitely not the best choice of words, but there you have it, eloquence fail.

"No, Gillian. We're the ones that get to stay alive."

"I'm not going to pretend I'm sorry you're still here." Without knowing I'm going to do it, I raise my hands to her soaked and curling hair, pull her toward me, pressing my lips to her jaw, her bruised cheek, her cold and oh-so-yielding mouth.

"Gillian, not now," Mel says, not pulling away.

The softness of her lips, the rising warmth of her body as it presses into mine… "Who knows if we'll ever get the chance again," I reply, and immediately realize my mistake.

"True." Mel stiffens and pulls away.

"Damn it. Sorry…" Stupid words. Stupid end of the world. I miss the feel of Mel already. With the rest of the world all sorts of fucked-up, why can't I at least get this one thing right? "We should get out of this puddle." I grasp Mel's arm, pulling her up with me and onto the center bench, or perhaps it's Mel steadying me. The eternal Bareilles-Halkey conundrum, who's helping whom.

"Sooooo…What now, dream-walker?" Mel asks. She lays her head against my shoulder and leans into me.

The feel of another living body, my living Mel, is totally worth the rising ache in my messed-up shoulders. Underneath it all, I can sense my body's exhaustion. Nothing on this save-the-world trip has gone as expected. "We find the Rampant and finish this thing. It really is almost over," I say, not believing a word of it. I'm so beyond trusting any Rampant-initiated plan.

Now that I'm sitting upright, I can see far more of this supposedly perfect land. A few dozen rounded beehive-shaped buildings are set a mile or two away from the shore. Above them circles a swirling cloud of what I'm pretty sure are yet more magpies.

"Gillian, you know what?" Mel says into the silence.

"Hit me with it."

"The first village of the Netherworld is pretty fucking underwhelming."

Mel's not wrong. The first village, per scripture, is the sun god Utu's nightly base. It's basically the border crossing of the Netherworld. It's also the Rampant home. I know this dried-mud village is just the first in a Mobius strip's worth of villages. Humans have lived and died for hundreds of thousands of years. The unseen villages they inhabit spill out in all directions, forever and ever. Amen. Still, it seems the entrance to the Netherworld deserves a bit more gravitas.

"Maybe we should eat something before we head out?" I carefully don't bring up the possibility of thirst. Like people on a boat adrift in the ocean, we can't drink the river water that surrounds us, and we can't retrieve the water bottles I lost along with the rest of my pack. Eighty something hours, that's how long most people can survive without liquids. Keep going. Hope it all works out. Walk forward into the unknown. Those are the thoughts I should focus on.

The Netherworld doesn't have airplanes or ATVs. Even those Wild-West-style wagon trains with their oh-so-helpful wheels are right out. What the Netherworld does have are dusty paths that radiate across the landscape, spider-web trails extending out beyond the chalk-gray horizon. In the Netherworld, if you want to travel, you go on foot or you don't go at all. Yet another reason to skip the sandals, even without Gilgamesh's Six Rules.

Mel hooks her backpack with one outstretched foot and drags it toward us. The pain in my right shoulder spikes even higher as she bends forward and starts rummaging through the contents.

"Power bar?" Mel holds out the rectangle of food and attempts a smile that doesn't hide a damn thing. She looks almost as lost as I feel. "The wrapping's still intact," Mel continues, when I don't immediately take the bar.

"Okay. Thanks" The sounds of crinkling wrappers as we open the packaging sounds almost alien in this ancient home of the dead. Eating, however, feels damn good.

"Uh, Gillian, what if the Rampant's not at home?"

I eye the bits of chocolate on Mel's lips, push the impulse to reach over and wipe them off right on down. "Then, I guess, we walk some more."

"What—" Mel frowns, incredulous, the crumbs dropping of their own accord. "Isn't there something with wings here? Or a desert sailboat thingy? What if someone needs to find their mother, or grandmother…or something?"

"They walk faster, I guess," I reply, going for the lame-ass joke. Cause, yeah, traveling some underworld sprawl on foot is total bullshit even when, or perhaps especially when, you have all eternity to finish the journey. Being with someone you love makes every damn thing better. No one should have to wait.

Kkkk ka kkkk ka. The magpie sound is coming from the direction of the village. A phalanx of birds has broken off from the circling cloud and is headed in our direction. Great. Just great. More Rampant magpie madness seems imminent.

"What is it with the gods and their fucking bird obsession?" Mel snaps as she shoves our pack back under the bench.

And then I'm shifting my weight, pushing Mel toward the bottom of the boat, while I brace myself—human armor—over her body, waiting, waiting, waiting…long seconds of waiting. But there's no attack. No shrieking flurry of wings and claws. Instead it's Mel's arms and legs pummeling me. The girl is gods-damn livid.

"I am a Rapture-trained living gods-damn woman. I am a fucking survivor, Gillian Halkey. I'm not some helpless princess. Back the fuck off." Catching me by surprise, she wraps her legs around mine. Mel is Camp Hallelujah trained, physical escape, like bloodletting, a well-practiced ritual. She twists, using my weight against me, and tips me into the puddle in the bottom of the boat.

"If you're not careful we'll both end up dead," I grumble as I scramble out of the water and onto the nearby bench, mostly just for something to say. It's clear no bird attack is imminent. The magpies spiral above us, close enough that I can pick out the white marks on the underside of their wings, but they're definitely not flesh-field crazy.

Mel, however, isn't about to let it go. "I'm the helpless one? How many times have you almost been killed on this trip? Huh? How fucking many?"

"Zero." I reply, lying my ass off. Once in a fight, I never can back down, and now is no exception, despite the death-world setting and the sketchy magpies currently circling our boat. "Anyway, some risks can't be avoided.

We need water." I cup my left hand, bend, and scoop it through the puddle beneath our feet. Before Mel can decide on a response, I press my hand against my lips, and against all supposed godly laws, swallow a few drops of the Hubur River. Gods, how long have we been without water? For a moment I savor the feeling of moisture on my lips and tongue. And then the flop sweat hits me, along with the clammy skin.

"Gillian?"

I open my mouth to respond, and then turn away from Mel instead and hang my head over the side of the boat. I look down into the shallows of the cove as I retch up the water, the Power Bar, the entire greenish-yellow contents of my stomach. My mouth burns. The back of my throat burns. My stomach feels like a tightened fist. But eventually the vomiting is done.

"Test complete," I murmur, looking back at Mel.

"Gillian fucking Halkey," is all she says, sounding both furious and scared, then she wraps me in her arms, rocking me back and forth, the two of us waiting for my shivers to subside.

"I didn't die, though. Not even close," I murmur, as I watch the birds wheel overhead.

Mel's snort is her only response.

It's in that moment—watching the Rampant's magpies—that it hits me. Never mind Gilgamesh's Six Rules, "Be careful of slippery god-types—and everyone associated with them" is this life's first-and-only rule. The fact that these birds were once human babies doesn't mean I should trust them now that they're the Rampant's reborn missionaries.

The Rapture feels more and more like so much childish make-believe. After everything we've been through, after so much loss, after Becca, Adala, and—how can I not cry?—Mr. Bareilles, Mel's continued survival, has to be the most important thing.

Dying is simple. It doesn't take much. In all these many worlds, one constant remains, "Stay alive." And so I focus, repeat the old mantra Pastor Edwins taught us at Camp Hallelujah: trust nothing, actively assess.

The most worrisome in a list of worrying facts: the small cadre of birds circling our boat is nothing but a zephyr in the living-magpie storm. Higher up, a thick stream of birds migrates across the Netherworld sky into that flickering, headache-inducing space at the far end of the cove.

"You seeing what I'm seeing?" Mel has noticed the same thing.

"Yeah." I reach into the pack for another bar as I try to cover the depths of my concern. If Mel and I are so gods-damned important, why is the Rampant still sending more supplies to his caterpillar hatching ground? Why is his insect navigation system still set to "go"?

"Leave the food alone, Halkey," Mel looks exasperated as she pulls my hand out of the pack. I try and fail to hold back a smile when she doesn't let go.

"Living girls," a woman's voice calls. "Living girls, remove yourselves from the water."

Nothing lasts forever, but could we at least have five minutes? I tighten my grip on my Mel's hand and turn, suppressing a sound somewhere between laughter and a scream as I take in our latest greeters.

I'm from Decatur, Indiana, and thanks to the almost-Rapture, up to now travel has been a total nonstarter. I've never seen an actual elephant up close. Despite all the Netherworld-and-death chatter, not one teacher or religious type has ever mentioned elephants in the lands of the dead. It makes sense, though. As Pastor Edwins drilled into us, upon death, all those with self-awareness are judged. Elephants recognize long-lost friends; they mourn their dead. Of course they made the list.

The elephant's ears are smaller than I expected, her skin more brownish than gray with a broad freckled trunk. But it's her expression that holds my attention. Though our greeters are still at least fifty feet away, the elephant's large hazel eyes don't waver as she walks toward us. Self-awareness has never felt so uncomfortable: that pachyderm is so obviously sizing us up.

Self-aware or not, it's easier to look at the elephant than at her rider. The woman's face just won't keep still. Whenever I try to focus my eyes slide away. Quick glances give me some information. The rider isn't using a saddle as she sits up there all ramrod straight. One more easy-to-discern fact, gods help us, this woman is clearly no human being.

"I've got this," Mel says, not looking down as she reaches inside the backpack. I follow the movement of her hand with my peripheral vision, though I'm careful to keep my head facing straight ahead.

It's not just that bacon she tossed at the flier. As well as the socks, the candles, and everything else we talked about, that blessed girl has packed her supplication knife, a six-inch blade, a sharp as hell and currently sheathed weapon she's carefully removing from her pack. All right then. Closing up the backpack only takes Mel a couple of seconds, slipping the knife into her back pocket even less.

Meanwhile, the elephant and her rider have reached the shore's edge. They tower above our little round boat. While the woman stares down at us with her skittering, wavery face, the elephant bends her head and starts drawing patterns with her trunk across the dusty ground.

For a long moment no one says a word.

"What does she want us to do? Pray to her?" Mel doesn't sound like she much cares for the idea.

Truth is I don't either, though one thing's for certain, whatever we do, we'd better get it right. Hard-fact time, the woman isn't just any elephant rider. She's a goddess for definite and sure, and only one goddess resides in the Netherworld: Ereshkigal, the goddess of the dead.

Up close, Ereshkigal's face is more than unsettling. I have a pixelated impression of a young girl, overflowing with righteous anger, and then zap, a brief flash reveals, not a girl, but the wizened features of an old woman with skin the texture and color of over-crumpled tissue paper.

"Remove yourself," Ereshkigal says yet again. Despite her petite frame, her voice is unexpectedly husky.

"First a question." I stare up at the woman, refusing to show how intimated I feel. "Why isn't the Rampant here?" I try not to worry about things like languages and comprehension. Try not to worry that we've entered her domain. Goddess, some corner of my brain mutters, a thought I brutally push aside. Fear is a tsunami. It destroys the ability to endure.

"Gan and I will guide you to the Rampant," Ereshkigal replies, not exactly answering my question.

"Great," I say, sort of meaning it. Actual words in a language I understand. Plus a plan: getting to the Rampant, instead of floating tired and alone. It's a Netherworld almost-miracle. But first I need that elephant to bend down so Mel and I can climb aboard its back. "We'll need help getting up there."

"No. You and your companion will walk. And you will carry the boat."

One problem averted only to crash straight into another.

The expression on Mel's face, I'm pretty sure it mirrors my own. Cold, battered, fucking thirsty as well, and yet here stands even more unnecessary bullshit. "You're kidding, right?" My words, my tone, it's like my carefully constructed mental filters have all been knocked right out.

I can feel Mel grabbing my left arm and squeezing hard, a sort of fleshy Morse code that I have no trouble interpreting: shut the hell up and calm down. As usual, Mel makes a good point.

Despite the flickering quality of the goddess's patchwork face, I can read her expression just fine. The lady is annoyed. "Gan cannot carry you," she reiterates. "The living and the dead shall not mingle." And then nothing more. She clearly feels she's made an irrefutable argument.

Godly arrogance just never seems to find its end. And idiocy. Inside me I can feel something slip and jump onto an unexpected track. "You're all nuts. That's it, right? The whole lot of you are nothing more than the King of Heaven and Earth's cruel joke on the universe."

Gan is no longer playing with the dirt. Her trunk's still as she looks at me straight on. The expression on her face: oh man, that shuts me right down. She's actually concerned for me.

There were maybe forty thousand Asian elephants before the Rampant's six siblings attempted to herald the end. I'm willing to bet at this point most of them reside down here. Kindness is definitely on the list of pre-Rapture lethal conditions.

"Gods-damn it," I snap after almost planting face-first on the hard Netherworld ground. I've tripped over yet another outstretched limb. This time it's a leathery hand gripping a mask. The ancient artifact glares up at me, all white ceramic teeth, turquoise skin, and golden eyes. For all I know, it's owner is doing the exact same thing.

"Gillian, let me take a turn, okay?"

I shake my head, take another step. "Not until we reach the village."

"You're being a complete pain in the ass." Mel looks more annoyed than concerned.

Good.

I'm currently dragging a bone-framed litter along one of the Netherworld's dirt trails—real dirt, thankfully—but all that dry earth doesn't mean there aren't also scattered corpses strewn across our path.

The dead may enter this world perfectly intact, but it's clear not all of them stay that way. Bodies lie about like so many plague victims—with one key difference: at least some of them are conscious. Off to my left, a mummified mouth opens and shuts as though determined to hold up its end of a never-ending conversation. A few feet farther on, a still-somewhat-moist corpse rhythmically pounds a jagged piece of bone into the side of its neck. Some of these once-perfect dead are missing hands or feet, some entire limbs. Whole or damaged, an unsettling number of them seem desperate to rot and escape their animated condition and this supposedly perfect land. Except, according to scripture and another one of my tests, they can't.

That water in the cove, the only water I've seen since we arrived, when I reach over and touch Mel's hair, flick the drops away, the nearby corpses don't even flinch—and they definitely don't start to break apart. Once they enter the Netherworld, it seems the Hubur River's waters no longer carry the same power over the dead.

Unfortunately, my still roiling stomach and this barren dusty land are confirming another river fact. The scriptures got at least one thing right: The Hubur's dead waters really won't mingle with life. Despite Utu's nightly dose of sunlight, the Netherworld is entirely empty of plants.

"This place pretty much sucks," I mutter.

"Yup," Mel responds.

As the patchwork goddess, Ereshkigal, decreed, Mel and I aren't riding atop her elephant, Gan, and we're definitely not walking unencumbered. Instead, with Gan's help, we've reconstructed the coracle for land travel, lashing the bones into a sort of raft, and then placing Mel's backpack on top.

A thick piece of hide is currently wrapped around my waist as I drag the raft behind me. "My turn first," I'd said when we started out toward the village, but pulling the litter turns out to be all thighs and as much shoulder muscle as I can manage. My body is biting out in pain. Meanwhile, my stomach lurches, still queasy from those drops of river water and a total lack of sleep. It's a good thing Gan is letting me set the pace as she follows from the rear. It's a good thing Mel is staying close.

"My turn." Mel says, grabbing my arm and giving me a look—*the* look—as I stumble yet again.

"No." I tense my shoulders and thighs, drag the litter forward, wipe the now steadily falling dust from my eyes. Falling dust? "Fucking magpies—"

"What are you talking about?"

I look up. There are no birds nearby. Our magpie greeters seem to have disappeared.

Glancing back. I see Ereshkigal still astride her elephant, eyes straight ahead. But it's the elephant, not the goddess, who really holds my attention. "Gan! Gods damn it."

The dead elephant looks at me with her calm elephant eyes and then sighs a long snorting, elephant-trunk sigh, feeding the dust plume that already surrounds her. It's not skin-and-hair rain falling on me. It's impatient-to-be-moving elephant dust.

"I'm not letting you pull that thing all the way to the village," Mel says. "If nothing else, you are *way* too slow."

"Like you could do any better." Maybe I really should let Mel have a turn…

And so it goes, bickering step after bickering step. At least physical pain is a purifier, dulling all those anxious thoughts. Okay, most people don't die perfect, but I was still expecting a steady flow of newly dead arrivals. The village ahead is maybe twenty huts tops, while our current path is empty of any travelers beyond our own little group.

"Gillian, are you even listening to me?"

"Nope."

At some point I notice a clattering, a shuffling against hard-packed earth that reminds me of my own feet, a muttered diatribe—not my own.

"Gillian—"

"If you'd just shut up for a second, you'd notice we're already there."

"Oh." Mel comes to a halt and I do too, as we take in the first of the Netherworld's blessed villages and the godly designed homes of the perfect dead. The beehive-shaped houses are formed out of adobe bricks and connected by yet more dirt paths. Up close I can see the rounded open holes in the buildings that pass for windows. There's no glass, no wooden doors, not even tarps or plastic sheeting to keep out the dust. It seems the Netherworld, despite its many immigrants and their wealth of experiences, is stuck in the past.

"Now we just need to find the Rampant's home." I start to take a step forward.

"My turn." Mel's standing right in front of me, glaring with that oh-so-beautiful, dust-smeared-and-exhausted face. Gods-damn her. "Right?"

"Okay, Bareilles. But no give-backs." Despite my words, I have a feeling my face totally gives me away. The pain in my shoulders is just the beginning. More of me hurts than doesn't.

"No give-backs." Mel reaches down and unfastens the strap from around my waist, tries to smile, fails.

If I thought prayers would help this all end well, I would damn well get on my knees.

I don't.

Dead people surround us as we follow the path through the village center. Mel pulls our bone-and-leather litter while I walk by her side. The reality of the place hits me in a way I hadn't expected. Some of the perfect dead sit in their mud-hut doorways. Others scratch games in the dirt or even hold hands. All fine. Just fine. I can lock those scratchy feelings right up. It's the ones who lie slumped along the edges of the dusty main street that are truly disquieting. All that hopelessness.

"Doesn't this seem just a little too weird?" I finally say. Not one of the dead has tried to speak to us or even tell us its name.

"I think they're afraid of her," Mel says, nodding her head in Ereshkigal's direction.

"Oh." It makes total sense.

The village dump doesn't announce itself via its smell. No rotten cabbage leaves, no carrot tops, and no marrow-sucked bones. Of course not. Dead people don't eat. Instead, it's the incredible glittering height that draws my attention. The midden stands just beyond the last hut, a rounded structure, taller and wider than any of the dead's beehive homes. Clustered around it are a half dozen pachyderms, busy at work. As we reach the far end of the village, I can see the movement of their elephant trunks. Some are rearranging the contents of the enormous mound, shoring up the edges and making sure the whole dizzying structure doesn't tumble down. Others are adding new things to the pile. Among the items I can make out: a blue Schwinn bicycle with rainbow tassels and a sparkling banana seat, thigh-high rubber waders, a plastic-limbed Barbie doll, a large color photograph of two people in wedding clothes, what looks to be Catholic prayer beads, and a beautiful gold-embossed book. The dead are often buried with special items. That has always been the case. But it seems manufactured goods, including those that emerge from printing presses, are quickly separated from their owners. Someone down here doesn't like change. And it's not hard to guess who.

In the end all that worry about finding our way once we cross the Hubur, all those nighttime discussions while Mel and I tossed beer cans out my bedroom window, were totally unnecessary. Once we pass the midden, the Rampant's compound is the most obvious structure in the Netherworld. For one thing, the dead stand upright ass-to-elbow, a crowd at least twenty deep. For another, despite the small group of magpies that visited our coracle, an enormous bird vortex still wheels overhead.

Some facts I know from my dream-time visits: a large moat separates the Rampant's house from the rest of the land of the dead, but in person, the crowd of supplicants obscure the moat walls and any view of the Rampant's mud-brick doorway. All I get are fragments.

It's bullshit, but I actually hesitate at the edge of the crowd. To reach the Rampant and get his help requires me to walk through all those sad—and leathery—corpses. I can't bear the thought of touching even one of the dead.

In the end, Gan maneuvers around me, allowing Ereshkigal to loom over this unhappy collection of her subjects. The bodies separate without Ereshkigal having to speak a single word.

"My turn." I reach for the leather straps tied around Mel's waist, try to scowl her into agreement. Fear doesn't mean I should let everyone else go first.

"Fuck off, Gillian. It's still my turn." Mel leans forward gently touching her forehead to mine before she turns away and starts dragging the bone raft through the crowd. I trail behind, the last member of our Netherworld parade. It takes just a few moments and about twenty rows of corpses to reach the moat, and then I'm standing next to Mel, looking across the waters at the Rampant's Netherworld home.

"Mel." I reach for her hand and grip it for all I'm worth. This is the first time I've seen the heart of the Netherworld with my actual and very-much-alive eyes.

"It's going to be all right," Mel says, as she squeezes my hand in return, an echo of Mr. Bareilles words I'd rather do without.

A magpie breaks away from the overhead swarm and lands on the earthen moat wall. After a hop or two, it adjusts its grip and bends its beak to the water, drinks. Huh. No retching. No trembling of any kind. The bird continues to look like one very living and very healthy magpie. So the Netherworld has some water for the living, which makes absolutely no sense. Then again we could do with a bit of unexpected good news.

"Thirsty?" I ask, as I tug on Mel's hand.

"Yeah, thirsty," Mel replies. She catches my eye, grins when I start to blush, though I notice she's blushing herself.

"Been practicing that pick-up line for long?"

"Well, you never know when it might come in handy. Especially around you." She looks at the bird and then at me, hopeful despite herself. "You know, I really am thirsty."

"Me too."

"My turn." Following the little magpie's lead, Mel lets go of my hand, and reaches down toward the moat water. Here are some things I don't do: I don't stop her, I don't scoop up some of the water and raise it to my own mouth. Instead, I watch as Mel holds her palm to her lips and tips that water right in. It is the most horrible of not-saving-the-princess moments. And it actually works out. Mel's skin doesn't melt off her skull. Her limbs don't detach at the joints. She just smiles. The nearby dead, however, back the fuck up.

"A living pair," Ereshkigal calls out toward the moat-protected house, clearly impatient to move this show forward.

Living pair? What the fuck.

Ereshkigal glances down at us from her elephant-increased height, but makes no move to explain further. It seems that as far as she's concerned it's announcement made, duty done.

"A pair?" The reply comes from the Rampant's mud-brick house. I'd recognize that voice anywhere. He rumbles. He wheezes. He growls. The Rampant's voice undulates through a series of registers lower than any human voice, living or dead, could ever make.

"Yes. A willing pair," Ereshkigal replies.

I'm not sure she's telling the truth. Willing is the last thing I feel. That phrase "willing pair" is drowning in all sorts of godly fuckery. Despite all my Rampant-fueled travels, I've never heard it before.

The Rampant's voice carries easily across the water and past the moat's low earthen wall. It sounds like he's chuckling.

"Gillian, are we fucked?"

"Probably, but in all the wrong sorts of ways," I respond. When in doubt, joke it out.

"Just so I know." And then Mel's untying the leather knots around her waist and leaning the closest end of the bone raft against the moat's wall.

"Time to finally sort this shit," I mutter as I lift the far end of our homemade raft and start to slide the whole damn thing into the water. And I mean it. It's time to float across this singular body of water and enter that eternal bastard's hidey-hole. It's time to wrestle what we can from yet another entrenched and arrogant god.

"Gillian, Emilia, I am so glad you've finally arrived," the Rampant says as way of greeting. Just as though I haven't realized all his dream promises are total bullshit.

"Ah. Yeah, about that."

The room, like the house, is circular. Its adobe walls curve upward, forming a domed, mud-brick roof. The Rampant lounges on his bone-bench at the far end of his home's single room. Just like in my dreams, his body is full of folds and rolls and crackling, dry skin. Our raft is outside, waiting for us to get the hell out of here. More importantly, Mel is by my side. It's totally selfish, but I'm so glad she's with me.

The odor of the Netherworld is weird to begin with, but inside this hut it's impossible to avoid the truth. The Rampant smells just like carrion: a sickly sweet scent, full of over-ripe fat. The guy really stinks.

Beside the doorway, the only other opening is the single round window that looks out onto the moat and the crowd beyond. Magpies, those once-dead babies, are everywhere, banking above the moat, migrating out to the Plains. They're even inside the Rampant's home. The birds settle on the ledge of the open window, circle inside the room, just below the building's doomed roof. They rest on the Rampant and his bone throne. The smallest ones, the newly transformed babies, briefly flutter on too-small wings, and then return to the ground and the lengths of human hide tossed about the hard-packed floor, a patchwork carpet of gray-green, purple, and orangish-brown.

Heading back home, keeping Mel and me safe, those are the thoughts I need to focus on. Soon Mel and I will leave the Netherworld with the Rampant in tow, and then the Rapture will begin, and we'll ascend, and everything will be better.

Right now, I can't imagine anything more stupid and naive.

"Emilia, Gillian, come closer," the Rampant says, in those same slow, rumbling tones he used in my dreams. He acts as though he has all the power in this world, which in a way he does. The fucker.

"And then what?" I don't bother trying to keep the anger out of my voice. Focus. Trust nothing. Actively assess. Something, something is grating at my skull, demanding I pay attention. Before today the Rampant never once mentioned Mel's name. I thought he considered her nothing more than my chosen companion, a nameless sidekick.

It's at this point, mid-concern, that the magpie noises outside start up again. *Kkkk ka kkkk ka*, followed by the cries of the unsettled dead: "Get down." "Stop." "Nein."

"Do it!" Someone calls out, proving yet again that assholes exist in all of the godly lands.

"Gillian." It's Mel. Her face is a mask of self-restraint. She's looking straight out that damn window, and now I am too, right at the corpse crowd on the other side of the moat.

Ereshkigal sits astride Gan, an elephant body length from the water's edge, no different from when Mel and I settled onto the raft. It's something else, someone else, who's causing all the commotion.

A man balances on the low dried-mud wall. He's wearing clothes frayed down to almost nothing. His long hair is matted against his skull, a tangle of dry straw. Gan might be carrying *the* goddess of the Netherworld, but even that doesn't stop the mass of bodies from pressing in against the elephant's legs. It's desiccated chaos. Some of the dead barrel forward until they're up against the moat's earthen wall, while others fight the tide, trying desperately to remove themselves from the situation. I can hear Mel's breathing as she stands next to me, the Rampant's creaking body as he shifts in his chair, but I can't stop looking at that man. His mouth is moving, though the cries of the crowd drown out his words.

"No. This will not stand. The living and the dead shall not mingle," Ereshkigal says. That psychedelic patchwork lady is looking down at the rag-tag man, ignoring the rest of the crowd. Turns out even in the Netherworld, being godly has its perks. Her voice, though quiet, carries over the madness, along with her rage. Both magpies and humans go still.

"Rampant, set us free." The man cries. His words are clear in the sudden quiet.

"The living and the dead shall not mingle," Ereshkigal repeats. Despite her harsh tone, Ereshkigal's old-lady face looks weary. She probably has no choice but to intervene. She is the King of Heaven and Earth's designated enforcer.

The man on the wall couldn't care less about godly rules. "Willing sacrifice," he calls, then stretches his arms wide, as though in prayer, and plunges forward.

"Jesus Christ, he actually did it," one of the dead cries—clearly a twentieth century corpse. The words overlay the splash of the man hitting the water.

"Gillian, look away." Mel's concern scares me, sure, but after everything we've already gone through, hiding from the truth is no longer on my to-do list. I watch as the supplicants closest to the moat push back, trying to fade into the crowd. Now that the deed is done, no one wants to be near the water and whatever's about to happen.

And then I'm biting down, air whistling out from between my clenched teeth, as I grip Mel's upper arm.

The man's body: it's like that chicken Mom boiled for one of the high holy days. Steam rises up. The skin and flesh melt off the bone, but not nearly quickly enough. His limbs are flailing as though he's still entirely conscious, if not exactly alive. All the while, a yellow oily liquid spreads out from the still unfinished skeleton. Like everything else in this supposedly perfect Netherworld, it's fucking unsettling.

Before the almost-Rapture, modern people used fire, immolating themselves to protest the Vietnam War, the russification of the Ukrainian, the lack of freedoms in Tunisia. This dead man's martyrdom may be forged in a ring of water, but it feels like it carries that same kind of power, willing sacrifices always do.

It takes long minutes before the skeleton goes still. It's only when the man stops moving that I allow myself to notice how Mel's holding me, our arms wrapped around each other, even as the tiding of magpies descends toward the water and picks through the remains.

We are in the fucking Netherworld. Where is that giddy sense that the dark days are over? Where is all of my stupid hope?

I turn from the window, pulling Mel with me, and look more closely at the Rampant's home. Those scraps of leather scattered across that floor are more than a flesh carpet. They're offerings. Each one contains a piece of writing. I read the words "help us" —likely scratched with the sharp edge of broken bone—on a nearly gray-green fragment, find it repeated again an orangish section near the doorway. "Help me," those two words fill the room along with others I don't recognize: "Aidake." "Membantu saya." "Giúp tôi!" "帮帮我吧." I'm betting they all mean the same thing.

Forget intimidated. Forget scared. None of that matters. "So what exactly is your plan?" I stare at the Rampant. Why had I ever believed his instructions? A creature like this, eons old and surrounded by desperate and dead supplicants. My specific human life can't mean much of anything to him.

"So many have sacrificed to bring you here," he says, seemingly concerned by my mood. Which is weird. By my count there are only three who have died: Adala, Becca, and Mel's dad. Since when does the Rampant care about such an intimate number of deaths?

When he finally decides to explain, the Rampant doesn't use words. Instead, that crazy nighttime oracular lump sings. His low bass burrows deep, searching and settling into my still-living bones. It feels like my entire body is thrumming in time to his song, as though I have no choice but to listen and believe.

And somehow, without the recitation of a single holy law or rule, I finally do understand his whole stupid arrogant flawed-as-fuck plan.

Forget about finally rolling forward and full-throttling into the Rapture. Forget about the living ascending to the King of Heaven and Earth's home on Nibiru. All those centuries and eons of existence have shown the Rampant one basic truth: the King of Heaven and Earth is an asshole. I obviously agree with that one.

It's the rest of it that needs some work. What the Rampant's been working toward with his dream messages and all the rest isn't the Rapture. It's an actual Netherworld transformation, a Netherworld that welcomes both the living and the dead. As it turns out, the baby magpies were just a test run. The Rampant is determined to change everyone's fate. It would have been sort of nice if it hadn't also been so gods-damn arrogant.

"So Ereshkigal can leave if we bring the living down. No more land of the dead means no more enforcer? Did I get that right?" Mel asks.

"Yeah." I frown as I grip Mel's hand even harder. Turns out the Rampant was singing to both of us. What if she believes in his bullshit plan?

His song. I don't doubt its sincerity. But the Rampant's skin is rough with centuries of dried Netherworld dirt. The guy was birthed along with his six siblings at the beginning of the world. The seventh Evil Messenger is as unlike me as those demi-god fliers or the King of Heaven and Earth himself. Of course the godly bastard got it wrong.

"Nibiru is a hard place, even for gods," the Rampant speaks slowly, as though he's convinced my barely suppressed rage can be logiced away. "Listen, child. As a willing pair you and Emilia can help so many others. With our help, there will be unguarded pathways down and true salvation for all those living souls. A world empty of gods including the King of Heaven and Earth"

"Except for you."

"Yes, except for me and Utu who still must carry down the sun. Gillian, all it takes is a willing pair and your parents, your friends, they will all be saved."

There's that phrase again, willing pair. I knew that term meant trouble. The Rapture requires its Rampant. Okay, it's clear that's not going to happen. The guy isn't about to move and, he's right, the more time I spend in the company of the godly, the less I want the ascension to Nibiru to begin. But the Rampant's new improved plan also has its issues, not least of which is the way in which he tricked me into traveling down.

Turns out after all those dreams, and all those months digging through to that crack in the world, my role isn't savior, it's more along the lines of drilling support staff. The Rampant needs a certain type of human helper, helpers plural, to create human-sized tunnels down to this world.

I gotta say, despite all the resulting good, willing sacrifice is not on my personal agenda. And I'm not sure providing Rampant with yet more supplicants is all that great of a plan—at least for the living people involved. Give him enough time in his transformed kingdom, and who knows what new madness he'll dream up. Omnipotent isn't a good look for anyone.

"No way."

"Nooo?" The Rampant actually has the gall to sound surprised.

"Hold up, Gillian, let's just hear him out," Mel interjects.

"Mel?" by which I mean "oh fuck."

Explanations are good, but the Rampant and Mel just won't stop talking. It's almost like Mel wants to keep him talking, and the guy, well, he seems happy to oblige. All those problems and his ingenious solutions have been bottled up inside, waiting for someone to share them with. Like the lack of Netherworld sustenance.

"Without plants there is no place for the living in the Netherworld. The new paths bring water along with a passageway down," he explains. It seems, among other gifts the King of Heaven and Earth granted him, the Rampant is a civil engineer.

"You have *got* to be kidding me." I say. "Once the living people arrive, they've got to figure out an entire land's agriculture? I suppose they're going to have to carry down the seeds and hoes as well?"

"Gillian Halkey, where is your gratitude?" Mel cuts in. "We will release Ereshkigal from her Netherworld bondage and end the madness above ground. Don't you want to help your mom?" What the fuck, it's like she drank from some godly cult Kool-Aid. Mel seems to have forgotten Adala and Becca and that one core truth: girls should never be sacrificed.

"It really has to be a willing pair?" Mel asks.

Willing pairs is a plural sort of phrase. As far as I'm concerned, my beautiful valiant broken-hearted Mel is getting to the heart of this willing-pairs issue way too fast.

"Willing pairs are how I created the crack you entered through." The Rampant replies. "Those particular pairs just weren't powerful enough to do anything more."

"But how did they get down here then?" I ask, pulled into the conversation despite myself.

"They didn't," Mel answers. Something about her voice. I can feel it. She's way ahead of me. I follow her gaze, look down at yet another magpie bumping against my feet. This one is so young it still has its down and pin feathers. Its new life as a bird has barely begun. And then my stomach is clenching, a weighted stone. "No."

"It's the birds," she confirms.

"It takes a vast amount of energy to create a crack and bring living water down. Those first willing pairs allowed the rest of my magpies to survive. They also gave me the energy to create the opening you needed to find your way down."

Mel is nodding her head, but her face is stiff. She is barely holding it together. The Rampant, though, doesn't seem to notice. Rigid expressions are his norm.

"So it all comes down to water," I say, playing for time. I have no fucking plan, not really, but that isn't going to stop me from trying.

"And unguarded paths," the Rampant replies. "The living require many new paths."

"Ah." Knowledge is like a free bird, a magpie dream, it behaves in ways the messenger never intended. Mel's supplicant knife—the one I've just pulled from her back pocket —is in my right hand. A godly sacrifice, willing or not, carries a special power all its own. I'm still deciding even as I raise the knife—yes or no? —and then, before I can analyze myself into paralysis, I'm diving forward across the room. My choice: his throat all the way across. My choice: a godly sacrifice toppling to the ground.

His cry as he falls is an earthquake of sound: low and power-filled and more than ready to crack the world open.

"Girls will not be sacrificed," I mutter as I look down at his prone body. Though he's not dead. At least not yet.

"Gillian!" Hands, living human hands, pull me back across the room.

Perhaps he can't believe in a world that doesn't have him in it. Perhaps when it comes to his own sacrifice, humanity no longer seems worth the price. Whatever the reason, the Rampant has started singing, dragging out something heavy with each of his notes.

Birds are everywhere, dropping from the ceiling, tumbling to the ground, more entering through the hut's doorway and window. Dead magpies like a godly plague falling from the sky. Willing or unwilling baby sacrifices, it doesn't seem that the Rampant much cares.

The Rampant's song is rising in pitch. Despite his sacrificial birds, the break is almost here. I can hear the creaking bones of the Rampant's chair as he bends forward, reaching out with one of his strange little hands toward me and Mel. Then there's a sound like an avalanche coming from somewhere nearby and a crack like the worst of our living-world's godly lightning. I turn as I hear the cries of the dead supplicants. Through the window I can see the moat water spilling out. When I look back at the Rampant splayed out on the floor, I notice a fine ash rising up with each wingbeat of the remaining magpie babies. Though he's still attempting song, the Rampant's body is beginning to disintegrate. A few more notes, the last of the bird bodies falling to the ground, and just like that the Rampant's gone, no longer on his hide-covered carpet, no longer in his mud-brick house. No longer.

The Netherworld, now godless for the first time. Well, almost.

"Water," someone cries. "So much water."

Underneath my feet, I feel the final movements of the shifting rock, as the earth gives way to those new paths down.

"I don't even know if it will work," I say.

"My knife. Your arm. Of course it'll work." Mel's bravado is like an old blanket, the same one I've carried since we were six.

That feeling pressing upward, those sobs: it's not the loss of Decatur, Indiana, that I'm crying about. Not even the loss of my Rampant dreams, my belief in his song. This time no girls were sacrificed. Instead, a rain of already dead babies fell to the ground.

Somehow I'm lying stretched out on the ground. My head is resting on someone's lap. Mel... The face that looks down at me is blurry through all my gods-damn tears. But the way she strokes my head. I would recognize Mel's touch anywhere.

"I'm okay," I say, a kind of a lie, but not entirely.

"You have a really stupid definition of okay."

Bravery time: "Just so you know, I truly totally love you."

"Gillian, of course you do, you fucking idiot." Mel says before leaning down and kissing my still-living lips.

I decide to interpret her words as "I love you, too." Decide that's one of the few basic truths I can count on in this new and possibly better world. Along with the warmth of Mel's breath, the softness of her lips pressed against my own.

"Soon, Gillian Halkey, the first travelers will arrive," Ereshkigal says. "And I will follow my brother, Utu, above the ground." Ereshkigal is standing in the Rampant's doorway, seemingly unconcerned by what has just occurred. She just wanted to assess the situation for herself. Reading the expression on that patchwork face is getting easier, or perhaps it's the depth of Ereshkigal's emotions: relief and possibly even excitement. After far too many lifetimes down here, Ereshkigal will finally be able to leave. It appears the method doesn't much matter to her.

"Wait," I say as she turns back toward the moat. I have so many questions. When living people die down here, will their bodies rise again? That's going to be fucking weird. And what about food? Can we really grow it with Utu's nightly sun visits? But Ereshkigal is done with me and Mel. She's crossing the moat and heading off to do what she's done for untold eons, greet her brother and the evening sun. Night is about to fall in the Netherworld.

"We'll just have to figure it out one thing at a time," Mel says in that oh-so-reasonable tone of hers, "the same as always."

And she's right. Trying things, getting it all wrong and then trying again, that's what it was like for everyone before the almost-Rapture came along. The Rampant's improvement, well our improvement, Mel's and mine, the gods, except for Utu, will be barred from this land. The almost-Rapture is an ugly wall living humans will never hit again.

In the end, what the Rampant ended up providing is a caterpillar path away from some dusty god's ugly idea of destiny, toward a chance at hope.

When Mel and I finally exit the Rampant's house and float our bone raft back across the moat, the sky has taken on an orange-pinkish glow. Night is here. Utu and the sun have arrived.

That's when the final Netherworld miracle occurs. Ereshkigal might be off to greet her younger brother Utu and his visiting sun, but Gan the elephant remains, waiting for us.

It takes just a few seconds for us to awkwardly clamber off the raft. Well, I'm all sorts of awkward. Mel as usual looks pretty damn coordinated and chill. "The living and the dead shall not mingle," I repeat as I look up at Gan, then for some reason, I start to laugh. And I swear to the absent gods, Gan lets out a snort in return, her trunk puffing air across both of our human faces.

In a move that takes me by surprise, Gan bends down and allows both of us to climb up, and then she's standing, stepping carefully as Mel and I sway atop her back. We do not fall.

Soon we're at a crossroads near the edge of town were the dusty paths lead in three different directions. Gan lowers her body again in a very clear request. I do as she asks, releasing my grip on her leathery flesh and sliding off.

Mel, mannerly to the end, pats Gan's flank in thanks once she reaches the ground.

But Gan doesn't turn to go. Instead, she stands on her massive feet, slips her trunk against my neck and touches Mel's shoulders. Never mind Ereshkigal and all her godly demands. Right now, it seems keeping us company is the elephant's only concern.

I reach out and touch Gan's dry, dusty skin.

"A purpose is good," I say. With the sunlight pouring down it's easy to pick out the mass of adult magpies still streaming overhead.

"One that makes sense even better," Mel replies with that classic Bareilles grin.

"Maybe we should try a new village. See who or what we find?"

"You know what really bothers me?" Mel asks.

"Just one thing?" I give Mel a look.

Like the smart person that she is, Mel ignores my bullshit and follows her own thought to the end. "I've been thinking about all those hatchlings. Human babies have a hard enough time figuring out how to crawl. But flying? Man, forget it. Those guys have *got* to be confused."

"Yeah. Okay." Encouraging young birds to fly, making sure they're all right. That almost sounds good.

I stretch, ignoring the ache in my shoulders—I know they'll heal—then I place one hand on Gan's wrinkled and dusty flank and the other around Mel's waist. And just as though we'd already talked it through, the three of us, Gan, Mel, and I, walk side-by-side away from the village, toward the rest of this dead world.

I can feel Gan breathe as she walks. I know she's dead, but it feels as though in this new world the quantity of life that one gives up is a personal choice, even for those without living bodies.

As we continue toward the horizon, one and then three and then seven adult magpies settle atop Gan's back. Perhaps they're going to help the hatchlings learn to fly. Perhaps they've just been waiting for permission to ride.

The pathway is open, and the people will follow.

A year, maybe two, I can handle the wait; the almost-Rapture has taught me that much. And if all those survivors need a little more convincing to travel down? Well, the gods know Mel and I will find a way to drag the entire living world into the Netherworld and end this godly nightmare once and for all. Truth is, we've already done much harder things. There's no way we can't succeed.